T0208952

Havana Dreams

A novel by Tom Boyd

BALBOA.PRESS
A DIVISION OF HAY HOUSE

Balboa Press books may be ordered through booksellers or by contacting:

Balboa Press
A Division of Hay House
1663 Liberty Drive
Bloomington, IN 47403
www.balboapress.com
1 (877) 407-4847

Print information available on the last page.

ISBN: 978-1-9822-3931-2 (sc)
ISBN: 978-1-9822-3933-6 (hc)
ISBN: 978-1-9822-3932-9 (e)

Library of Congress Control Number: 2019919336

Balboa Press rev. date: 01/27/2020

Denver, Colorado

Lawyer Wayne Thomas pulls up outside a Starbucks and looks inside!

Wayne: "Good, no other lawyers inside!"

Wayne enters, orders his favorite coffee and finds a spot in the back away from other people and with his back to the wall.

Wayne: "Wow it's been over three years since I've been here!"

Right before his arrest! Lots of lawyers hung out here because of the nearby courthouse.

Wayne's six day trial ended eight days ago! A jury found Wayne guilty!

Now Wayne was awaiting the length of his prison sentence!

Wayne had never been in trouble with the law before and was guessing five to six years as first time offender.

Then Wayne's burner phone rang!

Wayne recognized the number! It was Jerry, the paralegal from his attorney's office!

Wayne: "Hello!"

Jerry: "Wayne, are you alone?"

Wayne: "Yes Jerry, I'm alone!"

Wayne exits the Starbucks.

Wayne: "Hold on one minute, Jerry!"

Wayne walks across the street into a small park in central Denver.

"OK Jerry, go ahead!"

Jerry: "Well Wayne I've got some hard news that I've learned just an hour ago!"

Wayne: "From your special source?!"

Jerry: "Yes!"

Wayne knows Jerry and the judge's secretary has been hot for each other recently!

Wayne: "You know what my sentence is going to be don't you?"

Jerry: "Yes, the judge gave the orders to prepare the paperwork today for next Tuesday's sentencing hearing!"

Wayne: "OK Jerry, sock it to me!"

Jerry: "My guy at the FBI says the FBI is recommending 12 and a half years to life!"

Wayne: "Ouch!"

Jerry: "But, but your old crank judge McNamara is so pissed you didn't take a plea deal, he's going above the 12 and a half years and is sentencing you to 25 to life."

Wayne is so stunned, he cannot speak and sits in silence!

Jerry: "Wayne, are you there?"

Wayne: "Jerry, repeat what you said again slowly, and how you know it's true."

Jerry: "The judge's legal aid is doing the paper work right now on the sentencing. She has never seen the judge so angry, he missed three rounds of golf with his pals because of your trial."

Wayne: "25 to life, when Barry got eight years."

Jerry: "Says you're the lawyer you should have known better. I'm stunned and I'm used to some real shitty judges."

Wayne says quietly, "Thanks for the inside info, Jerry."

Jerry: "So very, very sorry, Wayne. You can appeal the sentence."

Wayne: "How likely is that decision on excessive sentencing likely to be reversed?"

Jerry: "It will take three to six years to go through the process and most likely I guess you will maybe have a reduction down to 18 years."

Wayne: "Oh my god, 18 years! I won't be able to see any potential grand kids until they're in high school!"

Jerry: "So very sorry, Wayne. I understand you're 50 now."

Wayne: "Jerry, I have to hang up now, I have to throw up!"

Wayne squirms in his seat and realizes what is in his pocket. It's a business card from his favorite cigar lounge!

"OK, now what to do?" Wayne contemplates if he should flee. "Where to? Shit, I don't have any cash!" There was less than $300 in his wallet!

Wayne has a small travel bag in his trunk with three days change of clothes and toiletries.

What country to go to? What country doesn't have an extradition treaty with the United States?

Then Wayne remembered his trip to Cuba four years ago! No extradition treaty with Cuba!

18 *months earlier:*

Ever since Chad and Billy were little T-Ball Kids, Wayne had helped with coaching. Sarah was a stay-at-home mom, driving the boys to games, bringing snacks and being at every game. Wayne was at every practice and every game!

When Wayne had to be in court as a personal injury lawyer was the only time he missed being there for his sons. He was a one person law firm.

Wayne, Sarah, Chad and Billy attended many baseball games and after the game, enjoyed meals in the gaslight district near central Denver.

Life was good! Home was a 4,200 square foot, 10 year old, four bedroom house on two and a half acres with a pool, a view, two golden retrievers, two cats, and a giant BBQ, with many evenings with several of the boys teammates enjoying burgers, swimming, and singing by a fire.

Wayne was a medium earner for an attorney in Jefferson County. Sarah took watercolor classes in Denver each week and became an accomplished painter, did custom watercolors for wealthy customers, for their homes and businesses.

One evening, one of Wayne's neighbors, Bill Garcia, comes over to talk. The men go out by the pool and fire pit.

His house is in the foreclosure process, he doesn't want to lose his home. Wayne agrees to help. Bill has brought his loan documents and leaves the thick binder with Wayne.

After Bill leaves, Wayne starts reading the documents and is alarmed at what he's reading, opens his cell phone and calls another neighbor, Grace Young, who works in an escrow department for a mortgage broker.

Wayne: "Grace, this is Wayne Thomas. I've got a loan document in front of me and wonder if you and John could come over for a glass of wine and take a gander at this mortgage document? It's from Countryside."

Grace: "Sure Wayne, John and I could be over in about 10 minutes. If it's Countryside Mortgage, it's going to be interesting!"

Grace and John arrive. John goes into the spare room to look at Sarah's latest paintings.

Wayne and Grace go into Wayne's office to look at Bill Garcia's loan documents.

Grace looks through the thick document, sipping wine and says, "Oh my god!"

Wayne: "Grace, what is it? What's the matter?"

Grace: "Wayne, Countryside is known for dirty loans, but this is a poster child for state and federal violations! Who owns this piece of crap mortgage now?"

Wayne: "Super Mega Bank, who bought Countryside."

Grace: "This loan is so dirty, Super Mega will probably not defend it! As a lawyer, you can jam Super Mega a little and offer the bank a new deal with a modified loan."

Wayne: "How would that work, how would we package the deal?"

Grace goes to Wayne's computer, pulls up home prices in their neighborhood, quickly has a current home value for Bill Garcia's house and points to the computer.

Grace: "Here's what the Garcia home is worth today! Lets work up a proposal to Super Mega Bank to reduce the interest rate down to 3.75% from 7.8%, put all the unpaid payments on the back end! It cost the banks around $30,000 to foreclose. The house has been hammered so much by area foreclosures it's slightly underwater. So let's propose Super Mega reduce the mortgage amount by $30,000. This will be a win, win for everyone and Bill's payments will be cut in half. Let's have a start date two months from now and lets put it together on an easy read, two page letter on your legal stationary and mention if this doesn't fly you might take further action."

Wayne: "Wow, do you think this will work?"

Grace: "Super Mega Bank won't want to defend this (pointing at binder), shit sandwich! I'll type it up right now on your computer."

Grace double checks her numbers and makes a proposal to Super Mega Bank of two pages and prints it for Wayne to sign.

Wayne: "Looks great Grace, now what?!"

Grace: "You need to find the shot caller at Super Mega. You can't give this to the local branch manager. You need to find the person who *can* make the deal!

Wayne: "Thanks so very much Grace, this has been an education!"

Two days and many phone calls later, Wayne found the man for Super Mega Bank in Dallas, Texas. Wayne e-mailed and talked with Mr. Styles, who was a VERY nice guy to talk to.

Mr. Styles: "I quickly reviewed your proposal for modification of Mr. Garcia's loan – here's my counter proposal: I will take $20,000 off the principle and do a new 4% loan, starting in 90 days.

Wayne: "Agreed, how soon can we have the documents to sign?"

Mr. Styles: "I'm sending you an e-mail right now. Documents

can be signed within a week at your local Super Mega Bank escrow office. Tell your client, Mr. Thomas we have a deal."

Wayne: "Thank you, Mr. Styles."

Mr. Styles: "No, thank you, Mr. Thomas."

Both hang up.

Wayne calls Grace and Bill Garcia and asks them to come over for a little celebration!

Grace: "Wayne tell me, tell me!"

Wayne: "Come over in a half hour when Garcia is here and I'll tell you both!"

Wayne, with a big smile, greets both Bill and Grace who have come with their mates. Wayne repeated all the steps to find Mr. Styles.

Wayne: "And here's the final modified loan."

Wayne hands everyone a copy of the e-mail.

Nancy (Bill's Wife): "Wayne, what will we be paying now per month?"

Wayne: "About $1,100 per month down from $2,100, this will save you approximately $1,000 monthly, plus they're shaving 20 grand off of the principle!"

All four are excited. Wayne pops a bottle of champagne and pours everyone a glass. All were very happy!

The Garcias could keep their home and at a monthly payment they could handle.

The Garcias handed Wayne a check for $3,000 and another check for $1,000 for Grace for her work and insisted they both earned it!

After the neighbors left, Wayne told his wife how good he felt about saving the Garcia's home and getting them an excellent deal. Of course, Super Mega Bank was motivated by not wanting to defend a toxic loan.

Wayne's phone rings, it's Bill Garcia.

Bill: "Hey Wayne, I have two clients for you on the phone!" Bill explained he had a relative and a co-worker who were facing foreclosure.

Wayne got their phone numbers and set times to get together – both were very excited with the settlement Wayne had secured the Garcias.

Now how much to charge? Each case would take a bit of time, and Wayne had no illusion the cases would be as smooth as the Garcia's.

Wayne met the next afternoon with Bill Garcia's cousin and his wife, and signed them up agreeing on $3,500 with a deposit of $2,000 and a promise from the cousin to drop off the loan documents the next day.

Wayne met Bill's co-worker and his wife at 7:00 PM. - the co-worker had his loan documents for Wayne.

This couple hasn't made a mortgage payment in nearly two years.

They signed up and paid the $3,500.

Wayne smiled to himself when he saw it was another Countryside loan.

He left with the loan documents and on the way home, called Grace.

Wayne: "Hey Grace, I've got another client that's in the works on a foreclosure. Have you got time to review the documents tomorrow? And make some money?"

Grace: "Yes Wayne, it's my day off. My boss has cut my hours down to 28 hours, and yes I'd like to make some money as these small checks I now get really suck!"

8:00 AM. at Wayne's home office with Grace:

Wayne and Grace agree on $800 fee for Grace, payable when she completed the whole proposal for Super Mega Bank owner of the current mortgage. Grace leaves with the documents.

At 2:00 PM, Grace returns to Wayne's with a completed loan modification proposal, neat, concise, and with the original loan documents with post-it notes on the illegal sections.

Wayne whistles.

Wayne: "Wow grace, nice job! What's with the post-it note?"

Grace: "Well, if my big shot at Super Mega Bank starts to waver, hit him over the head with the dirty parts of the loan."

At 3:00 PM., Garcia's cousin arrived with their loan documents and another check for $1,000 and a promise to pay $500 by Friday. Wayne thanks the cousin and writes him a receipt.

The cousin leaves.

Wayne pays Grace $800 and gives her the new documents.

The next day, Wayne is on the phone with Mr. Styles of Super Mega Bank.

Wayne: "Hey Mr. Styles, how are you? Ready to clear up another toxic loan? Did you get my PDF on the proposal?"

Mr. Styles: "Yes Wayne, I got it, reviewed it, nicely done proposal! Please call me Ben, OK?"

Wayne chuckles, "Yes, Ben!"

Mr. Styles: "I don't have much time Wayne, I have stacks of

these documents on a table in front of me, so I'll cut to the chase. Super Mega Bank will modify, but no $40,000 principal reduction, but will do $15,000 and a new rate of 3.75% to start in four months."

Wayne: "Ben, make it 20 and we have a deal."

Ben: "Done, nice doing business with you, Wayne. I'll e-mail it to you right now, papers to sign as per last deal. Bye!"

Wayne said, "Bye, Ben" but Ben had already hung up. Wayne was overwhelmed, another deal done! Wow!

Wayne called Grace.

Wayne: "Grace, good news! You did a good job, we closed another deal!"

Grace: "Wayne, this is so exciting! I'd like to do this full-time if you could get more clients."

Wayne: "Well Grace, I'll come up with an ad and put it on Craigslist tomorrow."

Within three days, Wayne's ad began running, and Wayne met with prospective clients about twice a week.

Some signed up, some didn't. Some were so low on money, they didn't even have the down payment on the $3,500.

Wayne lowered the down payment to $1,000 to get something started on the loan rehab – some didn't know where they had stored their loan documents.

Grace had quit her regular job. Her hours had been cut to three days a week. She now did the loan modification proposals for Wayne.

Another neighbor, Jerry Brady, was a CPA who for $300 per deal did a forensic accounting of some of the deals. It gave another level of sophistication to the proposed deals.

Wayne found it, took a lot of time to find the shot caller with each bank – there was a lot of turn over. Bankers often quit and were fired. Some new on the job were afraid to make a decision and did nothing! Would not move even when it wasn't in the banks best interest to foreclose.

Once a decision maker with authority had been found and a conference call was made, Wayne was getting a decent deal that day in about one out of three.

The other cases were held in limbo waiting a decision.

The banks were having more and more default of payments every day and had trouble keeping up with the foreclosure in the hundreds, then in the thousands.

Banks were so behind in their foreclosure paperwork, they hired temp workers to sign (forge) a vice president's signature on the foreclosure documents.

Later, this would become public as these foreclosure document signers admitted to signing the vice president's name, and no they had never, ever met the man. Some signers (forgers) didn't know what this vice president even looked like.

Even though they forged his signature hundreds of times a day, till their writing hand cramped.

All this was later exposed – bottom line – could the foreclosures legally proceed with a bogus, fake signature – signed by a $10 an hour temp employee not the actual vice president!

The dirty loans were the most likely to be modified, as no bank wanted to defend them and god-forbid, to have a court case. They would be toast in front of a jury, a sure loser of a case!

Wayne was securing 30 – 40% of modifications three to eight weeks after getting a deal started with full payment of $3,500 and full loan documents.

As the business grew, Wayne was finding which banks would deal and what banks wouldn't budge even when it was it the banks best interest to modify.

These clients were refunded their money except for $1,000 for time, effort spent, for these dead-end, going nowhere deals.

Some deals had to marinate for a while until more logical people with authority could make the deal.

Some banks were failing and had to be acquired by bigger banks and a lot of loans fell through the cracks, notice of foreclosure, public trustee sale would be filed – then later withdrawn when the bank realized property values had fallen to the point where the home owner had little to no equity in the home.

The home owner often then quit making payments on toxic loans – but would like to keep the house if a reasonable deal could be made.

Wayne and Sarah continued their weekends traveling with their sons to ball games.

Chad was getting a lot of looks from Big League Scouts when he pitched often three to five scouts with their speed guns.

Chad was throwing 90 – 94 MPH with a lot of control.

Billy was smacking the hell out of the ball leading his league in home runs. He had taken the PX90 body building, was really cut and after PX90, raised his batting average over 40 points. Billy was cool on the mound becoming the ace on his team getting lots of strike-outs low ERA.

Loan modifications were developing nicely and Wayne and Grace got a lot of satisfaction when a grateful family got to keep their home at a payment they could afford.

Then Wayne's ad caught the eye of a telemarketer, who was also offering loan modification.

His name was Barry Woods and he wanted to see Wayne for a couple of hours.

The next day, Wayne met Barry at his telemarketing office. There were 14 people in the room in cubicles on the phone answering leads.

Barry explained to Wayne the leads came from late hour inexpensive radio and TV ads – people would leave their phone number and the numbers would be put on roto-dial that could be triggered by the answering team.

Wayne and Barry go to lunch at a restaurant on the ocean with a great view.

Barry: "Wayne, tell me how you work your business, get leads, etc."

Wayne: "It's a lot of word of mouth and a small Craigslist ad, nothing as sophisticated as you have. I handle the settlement with the bank shot caller myself."

Barry: "How's that going?"

Wayne: "Well, some are taking longer working through the bank bull, but I'm settling roughly 30 – 35% of the deals we can actually make a presentation of an offer of settlement."

Barry is impressed!

Wayne: "Barry, what approximate percent do you get modifications on your deals?"

Barry: "Well, we could do better. It's not as good as I want it to be, that's why I wanted to talk to you! You see Wayne, some of these banks have found out we don't have an in-house lawyer. So they don't feel we have the muscle to make or jam them into a modification."

Wayne: "Sounds like you need a lawyer!"

Barry: "Yep, and since you know the business, you would be a good fit!"

Wayne: "What would be my responsibilities? And my cut?"

Barry: "First, we need to have an official sounding name for the company, and you would be president. Got any ideas?"

Wayne: "Well, I have North American Law, how does it sound?"

Barry: "Sounds good, and I can give you $275 per sign up that are funded."

Wayne: "Barry, how many sign ups are you closing per week, and how do you handle refunds?"

Barry: "We get 40 – 55 good leads for our closers who close about 50%, half are full pay up front, the rest on a three pay plan with data started when the client pays $2,500 or more!"

Wayne: "How are the refunds handled?"

Barry: "Ah well, we will have to work this out."

The men agree on the deal and within a month are looking for a bigger facility, with the recession on there are some very sweet deals on rental offices.

Barry and Wayne find a 10,000 square foot building four blocks from the ocean, 5,000 square feet on the ground floor and 5,000 square feet in the basement.

Wayne will have the main floor with the CPAs and forensic accountants.

Barry will have the call center in the basement and the 10 closers will be also downstairs.

The landlord brings in painters new carpet and within two

weeks, North American Law moves into the new digs – very impressive!

Nice meeting/conference room near the front with an impressive large table to meet with local potential clients.

Wayne's new hires were mostly laid off people from the shrinking real estate escrow offices.

Wayne was now quite busy on the main floor, but from time to time, Wayne would come down to the basement to see Barry.

Wayne overheard the call center people exaggerate (over the phone) telling potential clients that North American Law was 90% successful in getting people loan modification.

Not a true statement, and Wayne asked Barry to tighten up on his crew.

Barry: "Ya ya, will do!"

Wayne notices Barry doesn't care as long as they get the leads! He monitors the basement at least once a day and is alarmed with what he was overhearing.

Lots of exaggerations, all downstairs employees paid a base plus bonus per sale!

Wayne and Barry have a conflict. Wayne knows there can be no misrepresentation on the sales end, and caution clients there will be best effort but no guarantees. If all efforts are unsuccessful, a refund will be returned minus the $1,000 for time spent.

Wayne sets up monthly meetings with all downstairs call center and closers. He gives 15 – 20 minutes of don'ts on what you can't tell potential clients and makes all to sign and date.

Wayne is concerned Barry doesn't care and tries to impress Barry the importance of the guys not lying to potential customers.

Barry: "Ya ya, sure Wayne."

Wayne: "Well, this week we are going to issue over $80,000 in refunds to unhappy customers."

Barry: "Really, Wayne? Do we have to?"

Wayne: "Yes Barry, if any of those clients recorded some of the exaggerated BS the closers and call center gave them, we will be in big trouble!"

Barry: "That's why you have the ass eating meeting once a month?"

Wayne: "Barry, please tighten up downstairs, that's all I'm asking!"

FBI field office, a rented home in Denver, Colorado:

FBI agent, Jim Ramos and his partner, Jeff Robinson both work the Jefferson County and Douglas County area.

Ramos and Robinson are in their offices, an unmarked house. No signs.

Ramos: "So what's going on with our Mr. Barry Woods?"

Robinson: "Looks like Barry Baby is expanding and has hooked up with a lawyer, Wayne Thomas, who is fronting the deal."

Ramos: "What's the scoop on this attorney Wayne Thomas, any dirt on him?"

Robinson: "None so far. Seems to be a clean citizen – teaches Sunday school to junior high age kids. Two sons very involved in high school baseball – both kids have good grades and the youngest volunteers with ninth grade at his church. Good kids, good grades, wife water paints, she's friends with a Colombian lady who's fighting deportation. Wayne is clean with the Colorado Bar. No complaints.

Ramos: "So why is he involved with a scumbag like Barry Woods?"

Robinson: "Maybe he doesn't know Barry is dirty!"

Ramos: "Too fuckin' bad if he partnered with Barry Woods, he's fucked and is going down with that shit!"

Robinson: "Still!"

Ramos: "Still my ass! When Barry goes down, Mr. Wayne, father-knows-best is going down too! Screw him! He chose to go into business with sleazebag Barry Woods so down he goes too!"

Robinson is quiet and shuts up, looking at a photo of Wayne Thomas, with his sons and wife at a high school baseball game.

Ramos: "Tell you what, do a complete report on this Wayne Thomas – ballgames defending any drug scumbags, etc. and reach out to our inside (informant), give her say $400 cash and get an update of what's happening at the new location, number of clients, number of employees, etc. Better go in disguise, sit near at ball games, attend a watercolor class you like to paint, see what's up with the wife and her Colombian pal, Bella."

Robinson: "OK, I'm on it!"

Saturday morning, ball game at Golden High School:

Chad is pitching, Billy is in right field, five scouts are there with their speed guns.

Wayne, Sarah and about 30 parents are excited, it's a game against a nearby rival and the other team has 30 – 40 parents, boosters.

Sitting two rows above with his camera phone is FBI agent, Jeff Robinson with a very good fake goatee, baseball cap and sunglasses.

Agent Robinson is tapped on his shoulder by one of the Major League scouts - "Hi, you checkin' the kid out too?" The scout was pointing to Chad, on the mound warming up.

Agent Robinson: "Naw, I'm an independent reporter writing human interest stories on local players. What can you tell me about the pitcher?"

Scout: "Great kid, nearly straight As, only one B in two years, good family. Dad and mom are the couple four rows below on the left. Kid's got a gun for an arm, 88 – 92 MPH. Pretty good hitter too."

Scout: "The kid's probably going to be picked up by a university on a scholarship. Kid's 6'4" or 6'5", lefty, what's not to like? Need a pitcher with some heat? Watch the Thomas kid on the mound and watch his younger brother in left field. Hell of a hitter, hits about a home run nearly every game!

Good luck with your story. If you need more info, I've met the parents and I'll give you more when Golden is up to bat, gotta get down below with my gun!"

Agent Robinson: "Thanks, pal."

Robinson got a hot dog and a root beer and from time to time, would take pics of the Thomas family, the sons, Wayne, and Sarah. No one notices.

Chad pitches! Allows one single, strikes out two and a pop up ends the first.

Golden is up and Billy is the second batter, first batter walks.

Second pitch to Billy, smack! Home run over the center field fence!

"Wow!", cheers the scout. The scout turns and looks up at

Agent Robinson, smiles and gives a thumbs up as Billy rounds the bases. All scouts take out their notebooks.

Robinson enjoys the sun, the game and finds himself again sitting next to the scout from the Los Angeles Dodgers who also scouts for the hapless Colorado Rockies.

Scout: "Some talent in that family. Dad pitched in high school! Too many innings and when he was ready for college his arm was shot. He's devoted dad and lives for those boys, coached them through little league and Babe Ruth. The wife, Sarah is a stay at home mom who is quite a painter."

Agent Robinson: "I'd like to take some watercolor classes. Know where I might go around here?"

Scout yells out, "Hey, Sarah!"

Sarah turns and looks up.

Scout: "Where do you go for watercolor classes?"

Sarah: "Ricci Rinehold – Solana Beach every Wednesday morning from 9:00 AM. to noon."

Scout: "Thanks, Sarah!"

Agent Robinson: "Got it, thanks pal."

Agent Robinson exits the ballgame.

Scout: "So long, have a nice day!"

Robinson sits in his car, makes a few notes, gets a coffee at the local Primo Coffee shop. He eavesdrops on the local chit chat and kills some time reading the Golden Paper. He notices still a lot of foreclosure notices in the back.

Robinson remembers the Golden fans said they would be going to the local Pizza Hut after the game.

About that time, maybe within a half hour, Robinson drives a couple of blocks, gets in his truck, changes windbreaker, baseball hat, takes off his goatee, keeps the mustache and puts on a pair of glasses, whole different look!

Pizza Hut:

Agent Robinson grabs a mug of beer, a slice of pizza and relaxes on a high stool by a tiny tall table. He moves the second stool away from his table so he will be alone to check out the Thomas Family and their friends. Soon, the noisy Golden players and some of their parents arrive. The kids are celebrating – and Robinson is close enough to hear that Chad pitched six innings and allowed no runs, had 11 strikeouts. Billy also had a great day, a home run, a triple and a single. Golden wins six to one, what a great morning!

Agent Robinson overheads a man calling to Wayne Thomas.

Man: "Hey Wayne, want to go to the smoke shop in a half hour and smoke a stogie?"

Wayne: "Great idea, Bob, I'll be there-"

Wayne checks his watch.

"In 45 minutes after I drop the kids off."

Sarah hears this and says, "Why don't you go with Bob? Enjoy your smokes, take your time, I've got a painting to finish."

Agent Robinson leaves without hurry, gets in, checks his iPhone, and finds where the Smoke Zone shop is located. Again, he gets into his truck, gets new clothes, leather jacket, leather cap, sunglasses, and checks himself in the mirror. Good to go! He has fake business cards import/export.

Robinson gets to the Smoke Zone ahead of Wayne and his friend, Bob Jones.

Agent Robinson has a camera and mic in his leather jacket, gets four high priced cigars and a small pocket case.

There were four TVs tuned to sports stations and one TV on 24 hour news.

Robinson lit up his big cigar. Ah, what flavor, just as the cigar was rated high, tasty smoke!! Six others are enjoying smokes.

Wayne and Bob enter and are greeted warmed by the other guys. They are asked if they want to bet on a Big Ten basketball game.

Robinson turns on the camera and mic. He hopes to see some heavy betting by Wayne and record it! No such luck! $20 maximum bet!

Agent Robinson addresses Wayne and Bob.

Agent Robinson: "Hey guys, want to try a couple of good Dominican stogies?"

Wayne and Bob smile.

Wayne & Bob: "Sure!"

Agent Robinson hands over the small case.

Introductions follow, they shakes hands and both guys light up. Everyone enjoys the excellent smokes.

A real small celebration of the Golden High win, Wayne shows the guys a video with few seconds of Billy's home run and Chad pitching. The men wanted to see Billy's explosive home run played and replayed several times.

Agent Robinson had several minutes of video, said goodbye to the guys and left with more thanks for the smokes.

Agent Robinson leaves the Smoke Zone.

The Smoke Zone owner, Zack address the men in his store.

Zack: "Hey guys, I've got an announcement! Next month, I'm planning a cigar trip to Cuba, it will be five days of great food, good music, nicest people on Earth, and lots of free cigars. I guarantee a wonderful time, I do it three to four times a year. It's supported by the Cuban cigar maker who will feed us, give lots of $50 - $100 cigars.

Wayne & Bob: "Sounds good, how much will it cost us and how exactly do we get in Cuba legally? We thought U.S. citizens couldn't travel to Cuba."

Zack: "Cost is $1,200 a piece. We fly into Mexico and fly from Mexico to Cuba. We ask a Mexican official at the airport not to stamp our passports and again in Cuba ask them not to stamp our passports."

Wayne: "Will they do that and why would they?"

Zack: "Yes, they sure will and why do they do this? Well, it brings tourists to Cuba and they don't understand why our country doesn't allow travel. As far as the U.S. will know per our passports, we went to Mexico."

Wayne and Bob looked at the calendar and they liked the dates and the deal and would check with the wives.

Back home Wayne and Sarah discuss the Cuban trip. The sons had a very long away game during that time, yes it was a go!

Wayne picks up the phone, "Hello?"

Bob: "Wayne, are you going on the Cuban cigar trip?"

Wayne: "Yep Bob, I'm going. Sarah says I need a break."

Bob: "If you're in, I'm in! Sounds like this trip will be a blast!"

Monday at the FBI office:

Ramos, Robinson, and two other agents reviewed future possible arrests.

Ramos: "Let's start with our little friend, Barry Woods and his new partner, Wayne Thomas, the attorney."

Robinson: "I met with our inside informant and got a complete report on a number of employees. Right now, 48 and will get from her by end of the week the number of clients North American Law gets in one week!

Ramos: "So how is North American Law structured?"

Robinson: "Seems like it's an odd partnership between Barry Boy and his new lawyer buddy!"

"And when our shit hits their fan, who's ass gets the biggest poke?"

Ramos: "They're both going down, Barry is so dirty, he's toxic. We've been after him for at least three years, that's why we planted a mole in his office two years ago – made a check forging charge go away where she was facing three to five, now we get reports on Barry Boy and we give her a few hundred for her reports."

Ramos: "Robinson, what's Miss Mole say about our Mr. Wayne, the lawyer?"

Agent Robinson: "Small time, getting a few clients off of Craigslist."

Ramos: "So how did these two get hooked up?"

Robinson: "Our mole said Barry spotted a little ad by Wayne Thomas attorney helping people who are in foreclosure and called Thomas up and sucked him in. The mole, thinks Barry is using North American Law for legal cover and to hammer the banks.

Viva La Cuba:

Zack and 11 Smoke Zone customers from Denver fly to Mexico City – two hour lay over then direct to Havana – flew over the blue green harbor and white sand beaches with hundreds of people.

he had attended three years of high school in the U.S. and had graduated from high school in Fresno, California.

Driver: "Came back four years ago when his mother was ill. She's better now. He got the job with Mr. Soto two years ago – what a nice man. Please, call me Mike! I'm going with you guys to an exciting ball game tonight, then out for dinner, some music – I'll take you to some of my favorite clubs – you probably haven't heard this type of music before! I think you'll enjoy it a lot!"

The 12 men showered, put on fresh clothes and were given Primo Cigar baseball caps, Primo shirts in a creamy orange with the Primo logo. All quickly changed into the Primo duds. Mike explained leave dirty laundry in the small bags and it would be back and clean, pressed within two hours.

Cuban Baseball Gran Stadium:

The ball park was jumpin', music pumped from speakers everywhere.

Mike became their guide, he knew who the best players were.

Mike: "I played second base back in Fresno High in Fresno, California. Tried out to make the Cuban team."

Wayne: "How did you do, Mike?"

Mike: "Oh man, I couldn't come close. These guys are so good, they're like pros. In fact, one left last year and got a whopping contract with the Yankees."

Wayne: "I heard about that, a pitcher, right?"

Mike: "96 MPH, fuckin' heat, man. We all miss him, but good for him! God, he was good."

Bob: "It was some large contract, right?"

Mike: "87 fuckin' million, jeez!"

Wayne: "How did he leave Cuba, don't they try to keep their stars here?"

Mike: "Money, man! With enough money – a fast boat can get you to Miami in no time! Cuba has banned that hot shot Miami agent and his pictures up at all our airports to keep from from gettin' any more of our stars! Last time he tried to come here with a fake passport. He spent three weeks in a Cuban prison before he was released, next time two to three years. So I don't think he's coming back! He will have to be satisfied with his millions."

Mike laughs.

"Say Wayne, what does an agent generally get on a player's contract?"

Wayne: "Most likely 20%, so that Miami agent will get over 17 million as his cut."

Mike whistles. "Who could not use that kind of money?!"

Wayne: "Mike, do you have any other stars on same quality of the Yankee purchase?"

Mike: "We have two right now on this home team that could make any American Major League team. You will see them play tonight – one a pitcher we call, "El Chapo", is so exciting. 82 – 92 MPH but follows with a slider, curve ball, and a wicked charge up! Batters can't figure out what he's going to throw.

The other guy is a third baseman, pretty good glove but watch him hit! Wow, he is such a power hitter: We call him La Bamba, and the song by Richie Valen plays when he comes up to bat.

Bob: "Look forward to seeing these guys, Mike. Wayne and I have sons who play some pretty superior high school ball. All three are pitchers."

Wayne and Bob show Mike wallet photos of their sons.

Mike: "They look like big boys! Are they?"

Bob: "My son is 6'3". Wayne's boys are 6'4" and 6'5"."

Wayne says proudly, "Chad, my oldest, is getting interest from some major schools and Major League Scouts."

Music starts and everyone stands up for the Cuban National Anthem.

There are cheers and some hot music.

Mike: "Hey guys, want some Dodger Dogs?"

All the men: "What, really?"

Mike laughs. "Well anyway, the Cuban version of LA. Dodger Dogs a tad more spice, but good mustard is from Germany."

All the men order Cuban hot dogs. Mike goes to get the food, brings back large hot dogs and cold cups of beer.

At the game:

El Chapo pitches – he's an impressive lean. 6'4", righty who totally mixes up his pitches and confuses the batters, three and out!

It's the next inning.

Then second batter is La Bamba and the Richie Valen "La Bamba" plays loudly on the sound system – the crowd goes wild.

La Bamba stretches, warms up, smiles to the cheering fans, tips his cap. He's a powerfully built, 6'3" with Steve Garvey pop eye forearms. The second pitch with runner on first, La Bamba hits a solid double, driving in a run and gets to a second standing up!

Yep, Mike was right, these guys were good!

The men enjoy the games a lot. El Chapo pitches six innings, leaves with his team leading five to two. The replacement pitcher gives up two runs – the locals win five to four. La Bamba gets two hits out of four times at bats a double and a home run! The Cuban dogs were tasty and the fans were very happy. They left with La Bamba blaring out of the speakers.

Dinner after the ballgame:

All the Denver men were not hungry.

Mike: "No problem, let's go to my club and enjoy some music first!"

Wayne: "Will we be able to eat late, will anything be open?"

Mike: "Wayne, this is Cuba. Food is served till 2 – 2:30 AM. All our Italian visitors want and expect to eat late."

All three cars go to an underground club. The place is jumping, half the people are dancing – it's a totally more exotic somewhat dramatic sound. Mike gets everyone on the dance floor and encourages ladies to join them.

After three dances, the guys need a break and sit down and enjoy tropical rum drinks.

The men stay for a half hour and leave for dinner.

All 12 men got in their three cars and within a few minutes, arrived in downtown Old Havana. A huge high ceiling ex-casino turned into an elegant restaurant. Mike and Miguel steer the men into an elegant smoke lounge for drinks and smokes. Once all were seated in the leather chairs, menus were handed to each man along with pens to mark their choices of a wide array of dishes – some french, some Thai (Thai in Cuba?), some Russian, some German, obviously cater to some tourists – lots of seafood – the men marked their choices.

The room was well vented, soft lights, a fire in the fireplace gave a sweet smell (probably some pieces of applewood).

Mike, Miguel and the two other employees gave each of the men a small case with four cigars while wine was served.

Three musicians entered and began playing softly without singing.

The men enjoyed the cigars and watched a live boxing match on three large screen TVs. Little snacks were served until a waiter announced dinner was ready. All exited the smoking lounge and entered the huge dining room where four tables were set up with flower center pieces.

A large 15 piece orchestra with six barely covered, gorgeous show girls and singers were belting out some real Cuban songs.

Wayne and Bob both ordered chicken sautéed and Cuban slow-cooked pork with vegetables.

At 1:00 in the morning, all the men were so very satisfied and ready to hit their beds – ah, what an evening!

By 1:30, all were back in their rooms. Bob and Wayne shared a room – both agreed. The evening was everything and more that Zack had promised.

Music was incredible, food fabulous, but the highlight of the day for these two baseball dads was the ballgame!

The two men discussed the two Cuban stars and could they make it in MLB. Both agreed they probably could, but hey need to see another game to be more sure.

Wayne: "Night, Bob."

Bob: "Night, Wayne."

FBI Office:

Agent Robinson: "Ramos, our mole in North American Law tells me our Wayne Thomas is in Mexico."

Agent Ramos: "Take anyone with him? The family?"

Agent Robinson: No, he's alone – our mole only knows it's Mexico City and will be back in a week."

Agent Ramos: "Barry Boy still here?"

Agent Robinson: "Yep – last time he left the country was four months ago to go fishing down in Cabo, Mexico for four day, some fishing tournament."

Agent Ramos: "So Thomas went alone, he might be finding a place to flee if we bust him. See if our mole can get more info – give her another $300 and another $200 Friday. If we know where he's at, our contacts in Mexico City can follow him and get more data – no info, no extra $200. I don't want this guy to slip away when we put the hammer down!"

Agent Robinson: "The judge OK'd the wire taps for North American Law – we need to bring in about three more pairs of ears to listen in."

Agent Ramos: "Your all-American guy, Thomas might not be so clean if he's looking for a rat's nest."

Agent Robinson: "Right now, all we know is he's in Mexico City for a week, nothing more."

Agent Ramos: "Find out what's the deal with Mexico City?"

Agent Robinson: "Will do, and will get the Jefferson County ears down here in days."

Agent Robinson texts the mole to call him back and the mole returns his call in 10 minutes.

Robinson: "You OK to talk freely?"

Mole: "Yes, I'm outside on a smoke break, no one near, what's up?"

Robinson: "What's Thomas doing in Mexico City? Did you find out anything more?"

Mole: "I'll ask Barry, but I don't want him to become suspicious with so many questions."

Robinson: "Make it a casual question to Barry Boy!"

Mole: "OK, when do you need it if I can find out?"

Robinson: "Today, we need to put some eyes on this guy while he's down there!"

Mole: "Call you back as soon as I can!"

Two hours later:

Mole calls Robinson. "Robinson, I've talked to Barry."

Robinson: "What did you find out from Barry Boy?"

Mole: "Seems he's going to Mexico City with a friend to smoke some cigars – doesn't have the name of the friend."

Robinson: "All the way to Mexico City to smoke some friggin' cigars?"

Mole: That's all Barry knows, don't believe he knows anything more! By the way, I've got a couple of utility and gasoline bills."

Robinson: "Thanks for the call – I'll bring you by $400 in cash tomorrow morning at the usual Starbucks, see you about 7:30 AM."

Mole: "See you tomorrow!"

Agent Robinson walks into Agent Ramo's office.

Robinson: "Talked to our mole, Mr. Wayne Thomas has gone to Mexico City with an unnamed pal to smoke cigars."

Ramos: "Smoke cigars! Going all the way to Mexico City to smoke! damn cigars!"

Robinson: "I followed Mr. Thomas a couple of Saturdays after his son's ballgame to the Smoke Zone in Golden. He met a friend there named Bob, his kid plays ball with Chad, Wayne's oldest son. Looking at my photo of the game, etc. the dad's name is Bob (Robert Jones)."

Ramos: "What's the story on Wayne's friend, Bob? Jones, what's he do for a living, etc.?"

Robinson: "Don't know, but I'll find out, run a check on him, check for priors."

Ramos: "Why in the hell are they in Mexico?! Are they hiding cash down there? Chasing women? Damn, I don't like loose ends!"

The next day:

Robinson: "Here's what we have on Wayne's friend, Bob Jones."

Robinson hands his boss Agent Ramos two pages, Ramos takes the papers, quickly reads and scowls.

Ramos: "You hand me another damn' good citizen of the year – where's the dirt?"

Robinson: "There doesn't appear to be any! Pays his taxes, one speeding ticket, goes to church, light drinker, only smokes an occasional cigar at the Smoke Zone."

Ramos: "Check out the Smoke Zone, see what's up with them! Can we bust em for bringing in Cuban cigars? How tight is the owner with our two boy scouts?"

Robinson: "Those cases don't go anywhere, slap on the wrist. Just a little fine."

Ramos: "I know, I know – just do it!"

Robinson is on the phone with Ramos.

Robinson: "Smoke Zone is owned by Zack Sakie behind on some IRS taxes, paying them down each month, two speeding tickets, went to traffic school to keep points off record. Was given a registered letter warning him about selling Cuban cigars. Also, he's some big shot on the international cigar association that rates cigars, gives each cigar points. They meet two to three times a year each time a different country. Zack is an Iranian."

Ramos: "Now we're getting somewhere. Iranians are a tribe that doesn't follow rules very well."

"Iranians are not a tribe", Robinson thinks to himself.

Robinson: "Zack Sakie is a Christian and attends mass with his family at the big church in Denver.

Ramos: "check out his household see if he has anyone who has overstayed their VISA. Crawl up Mr. Cigar Big Shot judge's ass a little way – get me some dirt!"

Robinson: "OK, boss."

Robinson turns away and rolls his eyes.

The week in Cuba:

Two ballgames Wayne and Bob get the two Cuban stars to sign baseballs and posters – both players have again outstanding games.

More meals, more music, more cigars. Both Wayne and Bob are enjoying the vibe of the Cuban music. One afternoon, the group is taken up in the mountains for large-mouth bass fishing with guides all catch and release, but lots of photos and all bass are weighed before release. The men pay for nothing, they are guests of Primo Cigar Company.

Before leaving for the airport, Zack told the guys he was tipping our three drivers $50 a piece and it was OK with Primo. All the men did likewise. The three drivers were very grateful knowing Primo Cigar had OK'd the tip.

Mike: "Mr. Wayne, Mr. Bob, it's been a very fun time being with you both. Could you guys give my brother in Fresno a call and send him this money?"

Mikes hands them $300.

"He's been laid off and having a hard time!"

Wayne: "Will do, Mike. Consider it done!"

The return to Denver:

Agent Robinson and Ramos are in the luggage carousel area of the Denver airport when the 11 Smoke Zone travelers arrive. Zack has remained in Cuba to judge cigars and decide what scale of points to give the stogies, so buyers could use to make their decision. The higher the points, the better the smoke.

When the men are picking up their luggage, the agents have tipped off agents to look for cigars, there are just a few that are taken from Bob and Wayne are confiscated.

Robinson and Ramos leave the airport disappointed.

Bob: "Wow Wayne, I'm glad Zack is taking care of our purchases of cigars getting back into the U.S."

Wayne: "Wow, those custom agents sure had a shitty attitude, like we had committed a major crime over what, seven cigars?"

Wayne returns to see just in time, Chad and Billie's next high school ball game at home in Denver, Colorado. He comes to the game in the second inning, gives Sarah a kiss and greets his friends.

Sarah: "How was the trip? Tell me all about it!"

Wayne:" Tell you all tonight at home at dinner! What's going on with the game?"

Sarah: "Five scouts, two from the Majors, three from colleges, UCLA scout is here."

Wayne: "Is Chad scheduled to pitch?"

Sarah: "In the fifth through the ninth!"

Agent Robinson had a hunch Wayne would be there to see Chad pitch. He put on his disguise changed clothes and hat. Damn, he wanted to record more info on the trip, now hearing Wayne wasn't going to tell Sarah until tonight at home changed that.

Robinson is out in the parking lot and calls Ramos.

Robinson: "Ramos, think we can get a home phone tap on Wayne? I think he's going to tell someone about his Mexico trip."

Ramos: "Can't do right now, need some dirt at the North American Law first, then the judge might expand the taps."

Robinson: "Our mole tells me that Wayne fired his assistant and she is very bitter – this might get some ammo for our case."

Ramos: "Interview her, get a signed statement and give her say, $800 cash to help her out! Make sure she keeps her trap shut, hint there may be more money coming if she can keep a lid on this!"

North American Law continue to grow. Ads are working, more people are hired upstairs and downstairs.

Wayne hires another attorney to prepare a strong lawsuit against a hard assed bank with a toxic loan, who refused to help the home owner.

North American Law was on a roll, two employees under Wayne spent all their time finding who in each bank has authority to make a modification settlement. Hours spent, bad information, often employee of the bank had no idea.

Bank were laying off, being closed, banks being bought – no one seemed to know who the guy who could really make the deal!

Wayne was very busy training the new lawyer, the new people who did the forensics accounting – collecting data, calling customers to send in their loan documents, amazing some people pay their $3,500 and then drag their feet on sending in their loan documents, they have to be called every day to get them on the ball to send their loan package. Then the team would read each page and try to find the toxic pages and sections that were against state law.

Some loans were toxic, some were not! The non-toxic loans were a bit more difficult because the banks were not in fear of being in court in front of a jury.

Those mortgage deals had to be structured to make the banks realize they would be money ahead not to foreclose. The proposal included cost of foreclosure $30,000, plus the cost of rehab for the home – realtor fees. A loser for the bank, if there was a logical person with some common sense. The logic and the financial benefit for the bank was to let the home owner stay in their home, but at an interest rate that would keep the monthly payments low enough the home owner could afford.

Over 300 cases were modified with the banks to the home owners satisfaction. Another 500 were in process. Another 100 had not liked the deal and were getting $2,500 in refund checks.

Wayne had developed a casual friendship with another modification lawyer in nearby Jefferson County, Jimmy Bork.

Jimmy started like Wayne, with a few clients, saw the need, the potential, ran a few ads and wow, the business exploded. Jimmy had over 40 employees.

Jimmy: "Hey Wayne, how's it going?"

Wayne: "Going good, Jimmy. What's up?"

Jimmy: "We have three cases we would like to flip your way. They're close to you and we haven't been able to crack Farmer's Bank. How you doing with those dumb assed, ignorant fools?"

Wayne: "My impression of the new vice president was so new, he didn't have the balls to make a modification, so he did nothing but hasn't moved forward on foreclosure on our clients so far. Maybe he will grow a pair and start doing the right thing, but we have another Farmer's deal that is so toxic, it really, really stinks. We are going to bust this guy's chops, prepare a lawsuit, show it to him, try for a sweet settlement, let the bank off the hook and try to roll the other two into the mod in the feel good moment. Hope to make a friend!"

Jimmy: "I like your thinking, Wayne, good plan."

Wayne: "Thanks Jimmy, by the way, how many law firms are there doing the loan mod, stopping foreclosure doing what we are doing?"

Jimmy: "Counting you and me, there are 26 in Colorado and all are getting all the clients they can handle. The business is exploding!"

Wayne: "The banks have got to notice all the potential litigation."

Jimmy: "Yeah, it's got me a bit worried. We're poking the bear and what will the bear do if it's angry?"

Wayne: "They package a big ball of crappy mortgages, sprinkle in a hand full of solid loans, get that pile of shit rated triple A somehow and sell it off, earning a nice big fee! Now they're angry some lawyers are asking for modification?"

Jimmy: "Yep, the big bankers have a lot of power and juice in Washington. They want to sweep everything under the rug."

Wayne: "What happens to our clients if no one is representing them?"

Jimmy: "They're screwed – the feds don't give a damn about banks screwing the average guy! Wayne to date, how many bankers are in jail?"

Wayne: "None that I know of."

Jimmy: "Exactly! They pay a fine and that's it! Remember the senate hearing when Jamie Diamon of Morgan Chase testified?"

Wayne: "Yeah I saw it and couldn't believe it!"

Jimmy: "Real soft ball questions."

Wayne: "What a bunch of suck ups! I couldn't figure out which senator was going to kiss him first!"

Jimmy laughs, "Yeah that hearing should have warned us to watch our backs, we don't have any lobbyist like the banks and that bunch of spineless senators could sic the FBI on us!"

Wayne: "Would the FBI do this? They're supposed to protect the public!"

Jimmy: "Wayne, the FBI takes some marching orders from those senators and they get big campaign donations from the banks."

Wayne: "The FBI surely doesn't operate that way!"

Jimmy: "I'm sorry, my friend, but they do. Again, how many bankers have they put in jail? None! Bankers are buying islands, luxury yachts, while our clients are losin' their homes."

Wayne: "What a sobering thought!"

Jimmy: "Watch your back, my friend!"

Wayne: "Will do, let's keep in touch! Send me the three deals, might be good timing to jam Farmer's Bank!"

FBI in rented house ¼ mile from North American Law:

Eight FBI employees listen in and hit record when they hear any exaggerations or lies.

Ramos: "How's it going, Robinson?"

Robinson: "Going good, we have identified four of the closers that are continually lying or exaggerating. The other eight are really clean and go out of their way to point out there are no guarantees and are extremely clear in the closing presentation."

Ramos: "Do the four dirty guys close a higher percentage than the eight Mr. Cleans?"

Robinson: "That's what's interesting, there is no gain percentage wise for the four liars. Seems the eight have been coached by someone not to lie and they are more believable on the phone!"

Ramos: "Who would have coached these guys?"

Robinson: "It wouldn't be Barry, I suspect it's Wayne."

Ramos: "How about the call center people?"

Robinson: "Out of 28, we have two who continually exaggerate and on second shift, one person who also lies like a rug!"

Ramos: "OK, get data and record every lie and have them

printed and with audio so we can have a clear case to jam em' or take to a jury."

Robinson: "We have Barry on audio telling the closers to ignore Wayne's instruction."

Ramos: "Hold onto those recordings, I want them kept separate! I don't want our Wayne Boy gettin' off because of that recording!"

North American Law:

Wayne calls a meeting of all call center people and closers.

Wayne: "Here's the deal guys, you all were given do's and don'ts on what you can say on the phone! Even though you signed the guidelines, two of you continued to violate the instructions. Bennett, Keller, I've over heard you both talk and listened into your presentations. What didn't I make clear last meeting? You both have chosen to ignore my warnings so you both are fired! Clear out your desks right now!"

Bennett: "But we work for Barry."

Keller: "Yeah, Barry."

Wayne: "Yes, you work downstairs for Barry, but I'm responsible for this company staying within the law! You both are gone! We will have your last checks handed to you as you leave!"

Both men run to Barry go into his office, a few minutes later Barry confronts Wayne.

Barry: "Wayne, what the hell! Those are two of our best closers!"

Wayne: "They ignored my direct orders, I have to protect North American Law and they have to go!"

Barry: "OK, they're gone!"

Five days later at FBI rented house:

Robinson: "Ramos, something is going on at North American Law. No marketing violations for the last five days, everything has tighten up."

Ramos: "How many days recordings do we have no on each of the five targets?"

Robinson: "We have a minimum of 30 – 40 violations on each man."

Ramos: "Mr. Wayne, you're too, too late. We have your ass and sleazebag, Barry and five other shits."

Robinson: "Even if Wayne Thomas is being responsible for correcting the situation?"

Ramos: "Even if, even if, even if, Robinson your fair-haired, Mr. Daddy Baseball Dad is going down!"

Robinson: "How is it going to go down?"

Ramos: "Very soon, say in three days we go before a grand jury with the recordings. Our mole and the recently fired secretary, who is bitter. Shut down the recording on the call center right now! I don't want a grand jury asking about recent audios and finding clean presentations. Another important item our mole tells me; Wayne and his new lawyer are filing a lawsuit in eight days against Super Mega Bank. They have a slam dunk Super Mega Bank/Countryside severely toxic loan – that some dumb ass at Super Mega Bank has refused to modify. They are going to do a press release, TV, radio – when this hits we will have 30, 50, 100 more Denver lawyers going after this honey pot of litigation. We're going speed up shutting down all 26 lawyers. Also Denver bar has been convinced they need to jerk the licenses of the 26 lawyers once they are charged! They are a weak bunch and are so impressed by the FBI."

Robinson: "Isn't Colorado bar concerned about the rights of home owners?"

Ramos: "They never mentioned it once and neither did I, ha."

Ramos: "We are bringing our case to the grand jury in two days – get ready guys I want lots of boots on the ground."

The FBI raid is planned, Ramos explains:

Ramos: "The whole show! Helmets, face shields, vests, combat boots, lots of yelling handcuffing. A dozen include our five targets, Barry Boy and Mr. Wayne – take all computers file cabinets have three large U-Hauls ready. Inform three TV stations to stand by that morning and we have some hot shit for them. Perp walk Barry and Wayne out in handcuffs."

Ramos: "And keep the crew together, we're hitting that shit Jimmy Bork in Jefferson county the following day – the 26 lawyers are going down boys. This is the start!"

Robinson: "What about the home owners?"

Ramos: "What?"

Robinson: "The home owners have their cases in process what happens to their case who is going to follow up."

Ramos: "Let's leave that to the Colorado Bar."

Robinson: "If we seize the files and the computers, how can the bar follow up?"

Ramos: "Enough about the home owners."

Robinson: "I thought this was about protecting the home owner."

Ramos: "Think about the bigger picture, the country is trying to come out of the biggest recession since the great depression and a bunch of sleazy lawyers could gum up the recovery for years."

Robinson: "Is that what this is all about?"

Ramos: "Listen Robinson, you think too much! We have orders from DC to shut down this Denver bunch of lawyers who could clog up the courts and banks with lawsuits, and that's exactly what we're doing!"

Three days later, the big raid came off as Ramos planned. For more effect for the three TV stations, the FBI agents, 18 in all went in with guns drawn, while the cameras rolled.

Wayne and Sarah were with their sons in Scottsdale, Arizona at Chad and Billie's ball game – when the raid occurred.

Wayne's phone rings. It was one of his workers letting him know about the raid. Wayne's new attorney calls Wayne after being questioned for two hours, then is released after interview by FBI.

After the FBI interview:

The new attorney calls Wayne.

Wayne: "How is everyone? Who was arrested?"

Attorney: "Wayne, I can tell you more but only in person. I don't know if my phone is tapped! Better get a defense lawyer pronto my friend, the shit has hit the fan, watch your ass!"

Wayne and Sarah decide they will need a lot of time to discuss the whole dire situation and Wayne's probable arrest. They decide to have their sons fly back to Denver. They inform Chad and Billie. Wayne and Sarah check out of their motel.

Motel desk clerk: "Sorry sir, your card was declined."

Wayne: "Shocked as he knew he had plenty of money in that account, but hands the clerk another card, again, "Sorry sir, this card was declined."

Wayne goes to the motel ATM machine. All his accounts show $0 balance. Wayne confirms with Sarah, looks like the FBI has seized his funds. Over $170,000, even the money in his attorney trust account *scheduled* to pay doctors and hospital bills from a settlement on a car accident of one of Wayne's clients.

Wayne: "Shit Sarah, we are in so very deep and now no money to survive!"

Sarah: "Let's try one of my accounts and see if the card works."

The card works, whew! Sarah at the ATM gets maximum cash allowed and does it with her two other accounts!

Sarah buys the boys airline tickets home – goes to the ball field, gives the boys the tickets and some cash.

Back at the motel, packing their bags with the TV on, there is the Breaking News showing the FBI raid at North American Law! TV cameras film.

Wayne: "Look Sarah, at all the guns, helmets, combat boots, bullet proof vests! Jeez, why? Why?"

Sarah: "Our poor employees, how frightening!"

Wayne: "That's why they did it the way they did! Scare the hell out of everyone! Look, there's Barry in handcuffs and another closer in cuffs."

Sarah: "I never trusted that man! Barry always seemed sleazy!"

Wayne: "We'll have a long drive home and maybe we'll not go directly home but see my brother and sister first, and try for some financial assistance. How much money do we have that the FBI hasn't seized?"

Sarah: "About $19,000 and the money I have from the ATM here in my purse."

Wayne: "Sarah, please count it!"

Sarah: "$3,400 including money I brought with us. How much cash do you have Wayne?"

Wayne: "$600, that's all! So we have thirty grand to survive and right now we don't know what the bond will be."

Sarah: "Wayne, what are we going to do?"

Wayne: "Before leaving Scottsdale, we are buying five burner phones so we can talk with some secure lines – better believe our home phones and cells are tapped!

They stop at a phone store and buy five burner phones with 300 minutes prepaid per phone!"

On the drive home, Wayne calls his brother, a wealthy doctor, his sister, an attorney, and leaves messages giving a new phone number.

Wayne calls attorney, Jimmy Bork and gets him on second ring!

Jimmy: "Hey Wayne, how are you doing? Are you in jail? It's all over the news."

Wayne: "Not yet. Sarah and I are in Arizona driving back. I'm on a burner phone! Your phone is likely tapped!" The FBI has seized nearly all of my money – we are nearly broke!"

"Jimmy, they will come after you as the next target – about how much money do you have in your accounts?"

Jimmy: "About a million, plus!"

Wayne: "Get as much cash out now! Today! They want to make you broke and weak! You'll never be able to get back the seized money!"

Jimmy: "Will do, thanks Wayne, will do. And let's talk tonight! What number will I pick on my burner phone?"

Wayne: "Remember the place we first met, use the name converted to numbers – don't say it out loud!"

Jimmy: "Got it, Wayne. Thanks again, you're right. North American Law is number one in the USA and I'm second! Guess we poked the bear and the bear is trying to eat us."

Wayne: "It's happening, but I still don't believe it! I'm numb! Get your cash out Jimmy – today!"

Jimmy: "Will do, Wayne. God bless."

Wayne reaches his sister (who was also an attorney), who had seen all the TV news on the raid at Wayne's office.

Sister Betty: "Tell me Wayne, what's happening?"

Wayne fills her in – she asks for his new phone number and would have a defense lawyer in her firm call him within an hour.

The attorney calls Wayne.

Jim Cornell (Attorney): "This is Betty's brother speaking, Mr. Cornell. Call me Jim, I've got an hour set aside for this Wayne. Tell me every detail and I've got a brother in law who is in the FBI and I'll reach out to him to see why you were a target, that is if he knows."

Wayne and attorney Cornell talk for over 50 minutes – good questions are asked by attorney Jim Cornell.

Wayne: "Well Jim, what's your initial impression and how likely or how can I get off?"

Cornell: "You have poked the bear all right! The feds are letting the banksters slide and have chosen to shut down the attorneys doing the loan modifications! Without naming names Wayne, I'll tell you we had a banker quote bankster as a client one and a half years ago, who was afraid he was going to be charged, hid money in the Caymans, big yacht, condo in Paris, home in Spain – got a nice upfront retainer!"

Wayne: What happened?"

Cornell: "Never charged! But he retired, is living in Cuba, because the U.S. and Cuba have no extradition agreement. He's living it up, loves it down there – family visits through the Bahamas! Guys made a ton of money on toxic loan bundles and so far looks like the feds are going to let him slide – go figure! Wayne, I'll call you tonight, stay away from any place they can pick you up, okay?! We'll figure out a rough plan. By the way, your sis is picking up my fee for this hour! Talk to you tonight!"

Wayne: "Thanks, Jim."

Driving back to Colorado:

Wayne calls attorney Jerry Scrugs, the new attorney at North American Law. He leaves his number.

Scrugs: "Who is this?" Scrugs is uncertain, and doesn't recognize the number.

Wayne: "It's me, what's happening? Any news on the guys? Are they still in jail?"

Scrugs: "Barry has bonded out, surrendered his passport. The others are still there – TV keeps running the loop of the raid, the taking out of the files and now a close-up of the chains and locks on the front door. TV reports tonight interviews with three of your employees, this is the hot news of the day!"

Wayne: "Thanks, Jerry. Will keep in touch."

Scrugs: "When are you coming back?"

Wayne: "Will be in Denver tonight, please drive by and see if anyone is at our house!"

Scrugs: "I'm only 10 minutes away right now, I'll call you back in a few."

15 minutes later:

Scrugs: "Wayne, there are a couple of men sitting across the street in a plain looking car – seems like they're waiting for you. Better not come home till you're ready!"

Wayne: "Thanks, Jerry."

Wayne's brother calls their sister, she has filled him in – he's willing with some whining to put up one of his homes, gives Wayne the bail bondsmens' number of Harvey's Bail.

Wayne calls Harvey.

Wayne: "Hello, is this Harvey? This is Wayne, you spoke with my brother about a half hour ago."

Harvey: "Yep, I gave him the instructions, he's getting the papers ready. We are checking the value of the house, stay away from getting picked up till everything is good to go!"

Wayne: "Thanks, Harvey."

Harvey: "Keep your spirits up Wayne, we're here for you!"

Wayne: "Harvey, I've got a friend who might call you, he will need a bond also!"

Harvey: "Thanks Wayne, yes give him my number, have him memorize it or better yet, let me set him up ahead of time! That way, we can bond him out in two to three hours unless the bond is excessive."

Wayne: "Thanks, Harvey!"

Wayne calls Jimmy Bork.

Wayne: "Hey Jimmy, I've got the phone number for a bail bondsman, write it down. Or better yet, memorize the number. His name is Harvey."

Wayne gives Jimmy the phone number.

Jimmy: "Thanks for the call earlier, Wayne. I'm liquid, very liquid – retained a criminal defense attorney – now waiting for the shit to hit my fan. You figured out what number I put on my burner phone. Feels good to be able to talk free! Let's keep in touch!"

Wayne: "If nothing else we can try to figure out how to beat the charges!"

Jimmy: "It's going to be an uphill battle, my friend. The FBI is tainting the jury pool with all the TV coverage – makes you look like an Enron scammer! Have you seen the FBI interview with an FBI Agent, Ramos?"

Wayne: "Not yet, but hope to see it tonight!"

Jimmy: "Well, I've seen it three times already today and unless there is some other news story bigger – you should see it on a tonight's news. Agent Ramos does a pretty slick character assassination of you – even has two of your clients giving brief sound bite interviews of their opinions on how they were scammed and are still losing their homes."

Wayne: "Jimmy, please get the clients' names."

Jimmy: "Will do, I've recorded the interview."

Wayne: "Thanks, Jimmy!"

Wayne and Sarah arrived at sister Betty's house at 7:30 PM. Betty and her husband Ray, also an attorney have held dinner awaiting Wayne and Sarah!

Betty hugs them both – with tears in her eyes.

Betty: "Let's eat and try to relax a little – after dinner we can talk about the heavy stuff and about an hour from now, we will be able to reach our attorney friend, Jerry Scrugs!"

Wayne and Sarah are hungry. They both realize they have skipped lunch and only had one bag of Doritos each picked up at a gas station along the way.

FBI rental house:

Ramos: "Well guys, all in all a pretty good day! Good TV coverage, and though Barry Boy bonded out within a couple of hours, he wants to make a deal and blame everything on his partner Wayne Thomas. The other five are pretty shook up and none have bonded out yet. We played some of the audios and at least three of them realized they're toast. The other two are in shock, all are in single cells next to each other and we're recording everything said.

Robinson: "Barry Boy sure threw Thomas under the bus so quick. What a snake!"

Ramos: "Good work today men, get some rest. Same drill in Jefferson County taking down number two loan modifier, Jimmy Bork. He's got more money and assets than Wayne Thomas – probably bond out in two to three hours, so grab his funds and then one hour later cuff him and drag out the booking a little, buy more time in case the bank grab takes a little longer! See you in the morning."

FBI house all have gone except Robinson and Ramos.

Ramos: "Well, where is our baseball dad?! What does our mole say?"

Robinson: "They are in Scottsdale for two more days, should we have someone pick him up?"

Ramos: "Naw, we have a couple of guys checking his house, the neighbor is feeding the dogs. I'm sure he's seen the raid on TB and probably been called by someone! But we have nearly all his money. Barry has already rolled on him, we have our mole and we can do some reduced sentence deals with three or four others to test a lie, HAHA, I mean testify against Wayne – now he's fucked maybe he can coach the prison ball team, HA! He's goin' down!"

At sister Betty and brother in law's house in San Marino:

An excellent Thai meal (Wayne & Sarah's favorite) delivered from a nearby Thai restaurant, white wine too. The table was cleared, all were having some dessert, Thai ice cream.

Wayne phone rings it's defense attorney, Jerry Scrugs.

Wayne: "Hello Jerry, have any info for me?"

Scrugs: "Are you with your sister, wife and brother in law?"

Wayne: "Yes, we are all here, just finished dinner, and you are on speaker phone?"

Scrugs: "Here's what my FBI source tells me – there's a big push to crush and put out of business any lawyers who could jam up the courts and delay the recovery out of the Great Recession. Denver has 26 active lawyers doing advertising and getting a lot of clients from radio and TV ads. Wayne, you have the biggest modification firm in the U.S. and your recently filed against Super Mega Bank, is that right?"

Wayne: "Yes Jerry, four days ago we filed a lawsuit against a Super Mega Bank/Countryside toxic loan."

Scrugs: "The FBI has order from high up to shut down all the 26 lawyers and make an example of the raids on TV to scare other lawyers. This is coming from very high up and comes from the FBI director."

Wayne: "How high up does this go, this order?"

Scrugs: "So high up, we will possibly never know either from some powerful senators or from POTUS."

Wayne: "The president?"

Scrugs: "Yes, and if it's the president we may never know because the FBI director serves at the pleasure of POTUS. Basically Wayne, whether it's senators or POTUS, you have some very, very power enemies."

Betty: "What can Wayne do, Jerry?"

Scrugs: "I don't believe he has much of a chance. The FBI will make a plea deal with his partner and two or three others, have the trial in a conservative area where a jury will believe anything the FBI says."

Wayne: "Jerry, what are my chances?"

Scrugs: "Wayne, your chances of going against the FBI and winning is very slim!"

Betty: "Jerry, what should Wayne do?"

Scrugs: "The FBI wants to make this go away as quickly as possible, so stall, delay, request more time to prepare and try to make a plea deal."

Betty: "How much time? And can he save his law license?"

Scrugs: "He will lose his license, doubt he will ever get it back – even with a plea deal the FBI will want 10 – 15 years, maybe more!"

Betty: "What is the worst that can happen, Jerry?"

Scrugs: "25 to life!"

Betty: "What?! Wayne's never been in trouble his whole life, teaches Sunday school, volunteers with Little League kids!"

Betty: "Really Jerry, I'm shocked! Repeat that again!"

Scrugs: "Depends on the judge, the jury and how well the other defendants do on the stand. They are going to lie and say Wayne's a bad guy. If Wayne's lawyer tears up during their testimony, it could help but if Wayne can get seven years or less better take the deal!"

Betty: "Thanks Jerry, and can you handle trying to get Wayne and Sarah's money back?"

Scrugs: "Sorry, not me. It will take years and may not be successful!"

Betty: "Thanks again, Jerry."

Wayne: "Are you saying I shouldn't go to trial, Jerry?"

Scrugs: "I wouldn't, you could most likely lose a jury trial. The judge will be pissed and may slam you with so heavy a sentence, you won't see Sarah and the boys until your future grand kids are heading to college! So very sorry, Wayne! You got caught in the middle of some pretty powerful people."

Wayne: "Jerry, I tried to run a very clean program!"

Scrugs: "I believe you, Wayne, but if you get a decent plea bargain please take the deal! It's going to be the best you can do! Understand?"

Wayne: "I hear you, Jerry. Thank you!"

The next days' news, another raid. Jimmy Bork's law offices in Jefferson County goes down, TV crews crank out the suspects being walked out in cuffs. FBI in helmets, face masks, bulletproof vests. It's all over the news on every station.

Wayne's phone rings, it's Jimmy Bork.

Jimmy: "Hi Wayne, I've bonded out! Thanks for the bondsman. Harvey. He's great! Out in less than two hours."

Wayne: "What's your plan, Jimmy?"

Jimmy: "No plan for now! Thanks for the heads up – grabbed a lot of cash. The FBI got the rest probably right now, think I'm broke. Thanks to you I'm in a lot better shape! How you doin' money wise?"

Wayne: "It's real tight, Jimmy. I'm hoping my brother and sister will help. Probably have to go with public defender. The home we lease is owned by a guy out of the area found out he's an upside down and quit paying the mortgage. Now we will quit paying him – probably set to stay here seven to 13 months."

Jimmy: "Check your mail tomorrow or in a couple of days."

Wayne: "Jimmy, you don't have to."

Jimmy: "Yes I do pal – let's keep in touch. I've bought three more burner phones! Take care, Wayne."

Wayne: "Take care, Jimmy. God bless."

Wayne's temporary lawyer, Jerry Scrugs and bondsman Harvey meet Wayne at the jail and turns himself in, photographed and bonded out within an hour.

At the FBI house:

Robinson: "Hey Ramos, Wayne turned himself in and bonded out in one hour, has a defense lawyer named Jerry Scrugs from a big firm in Pasadena."

Ramos: "Find out the profile on Mr. Scrugs, let's see who we're up against and what his track record is. Does he go to trial or does he scare easily? By the way, did TV news get Wayne coming or going into the jail?"

Robinson shakes his head.

Robinson: "No!"

Ramos: "Damn! Oh well, we sure got plenty of TV coverage on the raid. Have the jail release Wayne's photo to the newspapers *all* the local papers, write up the release so the lazy ones won't have to do anything but run it!"

Robinson: "We got a lot of coverage on the Jimmy Bork raid, don't know how he bonded out so quickly?"

A week later, Barry and four others took their plea deal and were scheduled for sentencing in five weeks – a big splash in the paper.

Wayne found a package in his mail box, opened it up in the garage. Jimmy Bork had left a package of cash, $30,000 in $100 bills – wow! This would help!

Wayne sent Jimmy a text message of three words, "Thanks, got it!"

The feds had missed one cardboard box in Wayne's office and when he got permission to go into his office to get his personal property, he took the box home. Inside were 42 files.

He set up an office in the garage with two new burner phones and began to work on the cases. He still had his law license and began to beat up on some of the banks – who had not heard of his problem with the FBI.

Time was short, so he went for quick settlement and shortly had five homes saved!

Barry and the four others were sentenced. One got four years, another three years, the other two got three and a half years. But

Barry got eight years and was very upset! He thought he had a deal and expected when he threw Wayne under the bus he would get maybe two years! What the hell – should have gotten it in writing, damn FBI!"

Wayne continued to work the files, got seven more settlements with the banks. Four of the home owners still owed a balance and were so happy with the settlement, they wanted to pay the balance to Wayne. When he explained he wasn't with North American Law anymore, $4,500 came in from the four happy clients. Wayne cashed the checks at a check cashing service that charged a fee. He walked out with cash in hand. Chad's fees for tuition, rental in Santa Monica City College – he would be a starting pitcher. Billy continued to really smack the ball batting over 500%, lots of homers, triples, doubles. When the other team would play him too deep, he would hit a simple stand up single easy peasy!

Wayne and Sarah attended every game in Golden and Santa Monica.

Barry and the four other North American Law defendants went off to serve their sentence.

Just as Wayne was nearly ready to settle, six more cases the FBI and the Colorado bar struck 30 days later, his law license was pulled.

Wayne filled out paperwork for a public defender and was assigned a lawyer, Fred Reuss, who requested six months to prepare the case. The judge gave attorney Reuss four months to prepare.

The Trial:

The federal prosecutors and Wayne's attorney, Reuss picked a jury. The judge turned down a request by Wayne's attorney for a jury expert – but suspected the feds had a jury expert sitting with their three lawyers, whispering and passing notes.

The trial was a travesty, the four closers testified (lied) that Wayne had known the closers had lied to potential clients when questioned. In cross, they admitted they had signed Wayne's rules and warnings three times, but Wayne had told them not to pay attention (probably things Barry had said). The four admitted they had a deal with the feds to have a reduced sentences for testifying! The mole's testimony, it was all Wayne's idea to lie.

Feds made a big deal out of North American Law having over 1,000 clients and taking in over $3,000,000.

Trial ended, Wayne's court appointed lawyer failed or forgot to put into the trial the fact that Wayne had fired two closers for not telling the truth – big error!

The jury found Wayne guilty, sentencing in eight days.

The old crank judge, McNamara was pissed that this case hadn't been settled with a plea deal!

Sarah found a sale's job at a local large mattress store.

Wayne found a sale's job at a furniture store and delivered the Denver paper in the morning, getting up at 4:00 AM to run his route. Catching an hour of sleep, then going to work – commission only! Take time off when either boy plays ball. At one game in the stands, an old friend attorney, Gray sat with Wayne and Sarah. Gray's son was a very good second base man on Billie's team.

Gray: "So very sorry to see what's happen to you and Sarah – it's a shame. I was planning to hire three to four attorneys and do exactly the same thing. TV ads, radio ads, to help people save their homes."

Wayne laughs, "Well Gray, are you going to hire those attorneys now?"

Gray: "No way I want to have the FBI crawl up my ass! No sir-ree, I love money but after what happened to you, I wouldn't touch that business ever, ever!"

Wayne: "I understand, Gray. That's why the raid with FBI with guns drawn, TV rolling."

Gray: "Here's a little something that Jill and I want you and Sarah to have!"

Gray hands Wayne an envelope with over $3,000 cash inside!

Wayne chokes up, "What a friend! Thanks Gray, and thanks Jill."

Wayne calls attorney Jerry Scrugs.

Wayne: "Hey Jerry, got a few minutes?"

Jerry: "For you Wayne, I've always got some time. What's up?!"

Wayne: "You know of course I've been found guilty!"

Jerry: "Yes, so very sorry for you and your family."

Wayne: "Thanks, Jerry. Jerry do you still have some inside info with the FBI and or more importantly inside info on a very cranky judge, McNamara."

Jerry: "I have some real inside info on both fronts. My guy in the FBI loves to gossip, and one of our para-legals is banging the hell out of judge McNamara's legal aid. She's real kinky and he loves it! Will get back to you in say, two to three days. Take care, and so sorry I was defending a major drug dealer when your case came up!"

Wayne: "I understand, Jerry. Look forward to your call!

Sitting alone at a park bench:

Wayne doesn't know when he will tell Sarah! The sentencing date is four days away! What to do? Wayne gets up, calls in sick, calls his brother, gets his newest burner phone number! He drives home.

Wayne goes into his garage hidden at the bottom of his tool box in a baggie is his passport. Wayne takes a couple of Cuban cigars and walks out to the pool.

He lights up and stares at the passport that the FBI missed getting and the judge failed to follow up on getting it.

Wayne tosses a tennis ball to the happy golden retrievers, puts on a Dean Martin record. Man Dino was the greatest!

Wayne's brother calls – Wayne doesn't pick up. Another Dean Martin song comes on! Wayne sits and tosses the ball, lights up! What a smooth stogie! He grabs a legal pad.

"Dear Sarah, my love."

Backpack – baseball cap, fake goatee, Wayne drives to within 10 blocks on the red line train. He parks his car on the third floor of a large parking garage and walks the 10 blocks to the Red Line.

50 minutes later, Wayne is off the Red Line walking across the border. Mexico immigration cares little about a guy coming in.

In Tijuana, Wayne grabs a cab to take him to the airport – he's in luck there are seats available to Mexico City. Wayne continues to write a most difficult letter to his wife and letters to his brother, sister, sons and to his dear friends. Six letters in all are written and mailed once Wayne gets out of the plane in Mexico City. He only mails the letters when he knows he's booked on a flight to Cuba!

Two hours after arriving, Wayne is in his seat working on three more letters to his wife and sons trying to explain why he was forced to flee.

Out of his pocket, he pulls his friend Mike from Fresno and El Primo Cigar's phone number!

Once in Cuba, Wayne gets through customs and yes, they will not stamp his passport.

Wayne calls Miguel (Mike).

Wayne: "Mike, this is a friend, is there a ball game tonight?"

Mike is pleased, "Mr. Wayne Thomas! So good to hear from you! Yes, there is a game in about two hours, where are you at? Need a ride?"

Wayne: "I'm at the airport, can you pick me up?"

Mike: "Sure Wayne, what color shirt or jacket are you wearing?"

Wayne: "A green windbreaker."

Mike: "Look for me, red convertible, and Mr. Wayne, want to see a ball game tonight?"

Wayne: "Sure Mike, sounds great!"

"Wow, just got here and going to a ball game! Awesome! And a ride right away!", Wayne thought to himself.

He finally begins to relax a little.

The red convertible pulls up! Mike hops out, trots up to Wayne and gives him a brief hug and a big smile.

Mike: "Welcome back, Senor Wayne!"

Wayne: "Thanks Mike, good to be here!"

"Mike, you don't know how good to be here!", Wayne thinks to himself.

Mike: "Senor Wayne, where are your bags?"

Wayne: "This is it, Mike!"

Wayne holds up the small cloth carry-on bag.

Mike: "Okay, I'll put it into the trunk!"

He opens the trunk and places Wayne's bag inside.

The red Falcon convertible blends into the traffic leaving the airport.

Mike: "So good to see you, Senor Wayne!"

Wayne: "Same here, Mike! You say we're going to a ball game tonight?"

Mike: "Yes, at 6:00 PM, but before we will have a small meal-like snack, then the game and a real meal afterward – we will be joined by a star baseball player for dinner!'"

Wayne: "Mike, today you are the boss! Everything sounds good to me!"

There is a light, balmy breeze. Mike puts on the radio and happy salsa music comes on. Mike grins.

Mike: "You like?"

Wayne: "Yes Mike, I like it a lot!"

The men enjoy 5 songs and then Mike turns into a residential street goes a few blocks and parks in a front of a small house. People are eating at tables on the porch.

Mike: "These are friends and who are permitted to serve food and drinks! They are one of two to three hundred thousand that are allowed! I don't know, maybe more!"

Wayne: "Do these home cafes pay fees and taxes?"

Mike: "Sure, a fee upfront and taxes each month! But it's still a lot cheaper than the hotel and the big restaurants! And a lot of these places it's like my mom and grandmother made the meals! Now some of these little places have help from foreign chefs who help from foreign chefs who help with delicious recipes – French, Vietnamese, Thai – all new to us Cubans to enjoy! Ah, so good! Our tourists are beginning to pass the word around! We even have a little food review magazine of a few pages now! But it's getting bigger!"

Mike: "Before we go in, tell me why you came to Havana!"

Wayne and Mike exit the car and are greeted warmly by the owner Mr. and Mrs. Gomez.

Mrs. Gomez: "Sit here, Miguel!"

She gives Mike a kiss and shakes Wayne's hand.

"Welcome, senor."

Mike: "So what's on the menu today, my friends?"

Mrs. Gomez: "Ah Miguel, we have three choices for you today and a French dish, a Thai dish and a good Cuban dish with fresh pork like your grandmother likes to make! All very good!"

Mike looks at Wayne who smiles and says anything all sounds great and the smells are incredible!

Mike: "Could we each have a large plate with a taste of each? Remember, small. We are dining again after the baseball game."

Mr. Gomez: "Of course, good choice! And what do you want to drink?"

Mike: "Two mojitos, por favor!"

A few minutes later, two large platters along with their drinks arrived served by Mr. Gomez.

Mike whispered something to Mrs. Gomez.

Wayne wondered, "What's that about?"

Five minutes later, Mrs. Gomez and two of their children a boy and a girl, about 13 and 15 appeared with guitars. Other diners began smiling and clapping as the three began to sing! Ah, what voices!

After one song, Mr. Gomez joined in with his guitar. Beautiful music! The aroma of tasty Cuban food fills the air. Everyone is clapping, it is truly a magical hour in a small six tabled restaurant!

Mike paid for their food with cigars that the owners could sell along with after-dinner drinks for extra money! Wayne tips 20 dollars.

Mike went to the trunk of the Falcon and brought out a 12" x 24" wooden cigar humidor and gave it as a gift to his friends, the Gomez Family! Now the cigars will stay fresh and not dry out!

More hugs, ahs over the beautiful olive wood box that could hold 50 or more cigars!

Wayne laughs, and they both clink glasses.

Mike: "Tonight, my friend we will eat Cuban Dodger dogs, hopefully see our Cuban stars, have a great game, meet them in person, have a late dinner, smoke some stogies and let me figure out how to make everything better for you and your family! Fuck that judge!"

Mike laughs as well.

Mike: "Tonight, you stay with me."

Wayne: "Mike, you are truly my friend!"

Mike: "You got it, Wayne! My amigo. But no night is complete in Havana without at least an hour of songs, my friend!"

Wayne smiles at Miguel.

Wayne: "I'm in your hands."

At the game, the home team loses a close one.

After the game, Mike and Wayne go down to get autographs and take pictures of the players.

Mike knows El Chapo, the pitcher and invites him to dine with them and go to a club, afterwards to a music club. El Chapo says sure in Spanish, and they gave him a few minutes to shower.

Mike: "Sure, Chapo, we will wait by the exit number four for you!"

Wayne: "So Mike, do you know those guys well?"

Mike: "Yeah, I have dinner at least twice a month with El Chapo and La Bamba, they're friends. We have a great time together. Chapo will like being with you tonight, as he can use English lessons, and the Castro secret police are a little nervous because of the lessons. Afraid he might leave for the big, big money! Ha."

El Chapo exits, looking great. 6'3", handsome with long, curly hair, beautiful teeth and smile, looks like a movie star.

Mike and Chapo hug, introductions to Wayne. Chapo gives Wayne a big bear hug.

"He's so strong", thinks Wayne.

All pile into Mike's convertible. Wayne gets in the back seat to give Chapo more room.

Chapo is excited to practice his English and insists the three of them speak only English for the rest of the night! All agree, of course!

The men eat at French/Cuban restaurants. Excellent food and service, at many of the tables there lots of French visitors.

After the meal, the three men go next door for wine and cigars – baseball fans come up to Chapo to have their pictures taken with the favorite local pitcher. Chapo is very patient with every request, smiles for pictures, signs autographs.

Wayne is impressed, no wonder Chapo is so loved!

Now to one of Mike's favorite clubs, the music is so hot!!

All three get up on the dance floor. Chapo is surrounded by five very pretty women, each trying to get Chapo's attention! Chapo is all smiles, he loves it!

Wayne is getting sad! Back at the table, a band is playing a sweet, slow song.

Mike: "What's up, Wayne? Why so blue?

Wayne: "I just got here and already I'm missing my wife and sons. They don't even know I'm here yet!"

Mike: "When will they know?"

Wayne: "The boys and my wife should get their letters in about two days, I also wrote my brother and sister, and a dear friend at the same time, mailed from Mexico City to Arvada and Denver."

Mike: "It will take six to eight days, my friend. Do you want a pal of mine to call your wife or kids from the Bahamas and leave them a message that you're alright?"

Wayne: "Let me think about it, thanks so much Mike!"

Mike: "But for tonight, we will have a great time, okay?!"

2:00 AM – Three music clubs later:

Wayne thoroughly enjoyed the Cuban music! The three men are now done, ready for bed. They have spoken English as per Chapo all night.

Chapo has a suggestion all will spend the night at his house – Wayne and Mike agree!

Chapo's House:

A spacious hillside home with an ocean view and a large infinity edge pool, a pool side Cabana that was like a small apartment with two bedrooms indoor and outdoor, showers, a hammock and two fireplaces; one inside and another outside. Also a large BBQ, inside was a tiny kitchen.

Chapo shows the two men their bedrooms, gives them bathrobes and a stack of fluffy towels.

Wayne awakes in the morning. Mike has made his own bed and left. Wayne looks at his watch, it's 8:30 AM. Birds are chirping, it's a beautiful, clear day. Chapo is by the pool sipping a cappuccino.

Wayne walks out in the bathrobe.

Chapo: "Hey Wayne, good morning, my friend! Did you sleep well? Are you hungry?"

Wayne: "Morning, Chapo! Yes, slept well and yes, I'm so hungry!"

Chapo rings a little bell and a pretty woman in a maid's outfit comes out to take the mens' order, hands each a pad and pens to mark what they wanted for breakfast, it was in Spanish.

Girl in Spanish, "What would you want to drink while waiting for breakfast?"

Chapo: "English, please Norte de Americano."

Girl repeats in English the request if they need coffee, juice, or tea.

Both men request water, juice, and a pot of coffee.

Over a delicious breakfast of fresh huevos rancharos, grilled shrimp, and enjoyed the bowl of chopped fresh fruit.

After a little swim in trunks, provided by Chapo, the men slipped into the bathrobes and sat under shade on the veranda and spoke about their families.

Chapo, was the middle son with two brothers, one two years older and one brother one year younger. Chapo was 23 – he had been playing balls since he was seven and had been a star pitcher at

19 – getting better each year, adding new junk to fool the batters. His dad had died, when he was 14, his mom was in good health and he had a 13-year-old sister. He was very close to his family, saw them at least twice a month. Chapo showed a picture of his family taken two weeks ago. Chapo gave the picture a kiss.

Wayne told Chapo about his wife, his sons, Chad and Billy, his dogs, his home with the view, his love of baseball, enjoying being with his sons at Padres games.

Chapo knew about all the Padres players. He even knew their batting averages and ERAs!

"Amazing!", thought Wayne.

Chapo, big question. What brings you to Cuba, Wayne, my friend?"

Wayne decides to tell him!

His instinct is to trust this young man, who seems so mature and sure of himself.

At the end of Wayne's telling of his trial, decision to flee.

Wayne looks back at Chapo – Chapo has tears running down his cheeks.

Neither man speaks for a couple of minutes, then Chapo speaks quietly.

Chapo: "Thank you, Wayne for sharing! It's terrible what the judge is going to do to you, never to see your wife and sons again until you are an old man! It's so very wrong!

As a Cuban player, I don't make a lot of money – but I have this home, a nice car, a cook, a housekeeper, and two closets of clothes your size! We're both 6'3".

Please stay here with me, we can both help each other on English and Spanish. Please, live with me at my pool house. Help yourself to any clothes you want. Fans are always giving me free stuff, shoes, sports coats, so much free stuff that two to three times a year, I give it away!

Please stay and live with me and we can figure out how to have your Sarah, Chad and Billy visit!

If you are bored, there are some local kids nine to 13 who need a coach, as their coach had a heart attack.

Other days, you can come down to practice and meet the rest of the players.

Wayne is stunned! What a fine young man! Mature beyond his years!

Wayne: "You sure, Chapo?"

Chapo: "Yes, very sure!"

Wayne: "Thanks so much, I accept your kind offer!"

Chapo is off the next two days.

Chapo: "Wayne, I'd like you to meet my family, my friend!"

Wayne: "I'd like that Chapo – I've got five letters I need to send back to the States, any ideas on how to do this without giving up where they came from?"

Chapo: "How about having Mike ask one of his cigar tour customers to mail them from say, Germany, France, Spain, ha, drive the feds crazy!"

Wayne: "I need to tell Mike I'm living here."

Chapo: "Already told him, he likes this idea of you living here a lot. I'll call him to pick up your letters.

FBI rented house Denver Colorado:

Robinson: "Ramos, we haven't seen Wayne Thomas for three days, not at work, not at home!"

Ramos: "Think he jumped bail and fled?"

Robinson: "Another problem, if he fled, we failed to secure his passport."

Ramos, very angry, "What the fuck?! How did that happen?"

Robinson: "The agent didn't follow up! Fell through the cracks."

Ramos: "Okay, okay, let's say he fled. Where would he go? Any ideas? Let's brainstorm! Anything on phone taps? Let's tap his brother's phone."

Robinson: "It appears he and his wife and sons are all using burner phones."

Ramos: "Check all airlines in the dates when he could have used his passport, get back to me in two hours."

Two hours later:

Robinson: "Well, we found out Wayne flew four days ago from Tijuana to Mexico City."

Ramos: "So, he's in Mexico?"

Robinson: "Maybe, maybe."

Ramos: "Why the maybe? What are you thinking?"

Robinson: "Our men in Mexico City have Wayne exiting the Tijuana plane, and a tape of him leaving the plane, he has on a disguise goatee, here it is on my phone!"

Robinson shows Ramos his phone.

Ramos: "Any info on any other plane he was on leaving Mexico City? Cabo? Anything?"

Robinson: "So far, nothing!"

Ramos: "Have our Mexico City agent check the video for the four hours after Wayne Thomas landed. We know what he looked like and has a red ball cap, unless he ditched it! See if he got on another flight!"

Robinson: "Will do, boss!"

Ramos: "And let's pronto tap the brother's phone, but not the lawyer sister."

Three hours later:

Robinson: "Ramos, our Mexico City agent sent this tape – Wayne ditched his cap, pulled off the goatee and was walking around, getting a beer and killing time."

Ramos: "He's waiting for his flight out somewhere, but where?"

Robinson: "Don't know yet, but we'll try to find out!"

Back in Havana:

Wayne and Chapo are in Chapo's 1956 Chevy convertible, going to visit Chapo's family one hour away in a small village.

Chapo: "I gave Mike your letters, good timing. He was heading to the airport with a large group of clients and asked five different guys from five different countries to mail the letters when they got home. Holland, Germany, Spain, England, and Ireland. Let them chase those leads, ha!"

A light rain, Chapo puts the top up!

Wayne meets Chapo's warm family.

It's Thursday and the older brother, Juan, is at work at a nearby resort where he works as a waiter.

Maria, the mother is 46, close to Sarah's age. She is beautiful. The 13 year old sister is in school. Carlos is at home working in the vegetable garden in the back.

Carlos and Chapo hug. Chapo shoves a wad of cash into his brother's pocket.

Chapo: "For the family."

Carlos: "Si, Chapo!"

A very nice late lunch: baked chicken, fresh veggies from the garden, new tortillas, simple food but oh so good!

Older brother, Juan has a break from the lunch crowd and comes home on a Vespa scooter. He's warmly introduced as Chapo's best friend. Juan is 6'2" and is nicely groomed, tanned and fit. Speaks perfect English and French!

Wayne is thinking, "Bet the French babes go for this Latin lover!"

Juan is happy, made lots of tips at lunch. American dollars go a long way in Cuba!

Chapo and Wayne visit the chicken coop and collect 14 eggs family will use some and share the rest with some poor neighbors.

Sister Lupe comes home, jumps into Chapo's arms. She is the spoiled baby in the family and everyone adores her.

Lupe: "Chapo, can you stay? Please, please?"

Chapo: "No, my little kitten. I can't, so sorry."

Lupe pouts a little, then smiles.

Lupe: "Stay for cake, then?"

Juan brought one back from work.

Chapo: "Okay Lupe, we'll stay for one slice! Meet my friend, Wayne."

A week later at the Thomas home:

Sarah is interviewed by two FBI agents who try to threaten her, it has the opposite effect.

Sarah: "You two are despicable, coming in here trying to scare me!"

FBI Agent: "You will be charged with obstruction of justice if you aid Wayne in any way-"

Sarah: "Bite me, you goons."

The agents leave, red faced!

Sarah gets the mail, she has a letter from Germany? She opens the letter, it's from Wayne. She sits down and tears run down her face and begins to read the letter. Sobs, one of the dogs is concerned and lays its head on her lap.

"My dearest,

Please understand this is the hardest thing I've had to do in my life – had real solid info that the judge was giving me 25 to life and left me no choice! Please forgive me for not telling you what I was going to do, but you discuss everything your pal, Marta – and she might have spilled the beans.

Please tell the boys I love them a lot. I'm safe, secure, and have friends I can trust and would love to see you, hold you. I will set it up somehow. You will need to come to me! I've stashed some cash from a friend in our favorite hiding place – you know where it is!

Give the boys a hug from me! I've written them both a letter.

I'm in a warm place, safe, secure and teaching 9 – 13-year-olds baseball, love these kids. Remember when Chad and Billy were little – you were such a great mother making snacks, cookies for the team, having the team over for hot dogs and a swim.

I'll see you soon, my dear, as soon as the FBI realizes they can't touch me here.

Where I'm at, there is no extradition treaty. Tell my brother I'm sorry he's going to lose one of his houses to the bond company. So very sorry, tell them I love them. I sent a letter but don't know if he's gotten it! Keep using the special phones.

Hope your work is going well, pet the dogs, throw the tennis ball. Please take some pictures of you and the boys by the pool with with the dogs so I can have them in my wallet!

I'll send you a picture that will show you how well I'm being cared for, being well fed, living in a small house that's very clean. I eat well, but miss your delicious meals.

Every time I hear a good song, I think of how much you would enjoy hearing this tune!

Miss you and the boys, our dogs, our friends, our wonderful priest, my little Sunday school kids, but where I'm at is for the best compared to 25 years to life in a federal prison. Have you heard of any bankers being sent to jail? Don't bother answering that, I know the answer. I know there are none!

Love you, miss you,
-Wayne"

At the FBI house:

Ramos, Robinson, and two other agents are also looking at the same exact letter from Wayne to Sarah.

Ramos: "First, let's discuss Germany – is Wayne in Germany? Any opinions in the room?"

Agent #1: "Don't believe he's in Germany, maybe passing through."

Agent #2: "Might be in Germany with a fake passport."

Robinson: "Our agents in Germany found no Wayne Thomas entering Germany."

Ramos: "Remember this disguise in Mexico City! Any more info from our guys in Mexico City review the tapes from the day he landed and was spotted – what entrance to another plane was he going into?"

Agent #1: "If he knew we had video going, he could have gone into one of the gift shops, changed jacket, different color, bought a hat or a hoodie, then went to his next flight and we wouldn't know it was him."

Ramos: "So have you expressed this theory to our guys in Mexico City?"

Agent #1: "Yes, they are following the tape on Wayne and have all his stops wandering around the airport. I expect to hear from them in a few minutes."

The phone rings, it's their Mexico City guy.

Agent #1: "Yes, I'm walking to our computer a few feet away."

All the agents look at the large computer screen of Wayne wandering around the huge airport. Wayne goes into a store, doesn't exit, except a tall man wearing a hoodie, a jean jacket, a floppy hat and sunglasses.

Ramos: "That's Wayne, I bet it's him. Let's see where this guy in the hoodie goes, what plane he's getting on."

The camera follows Wayne – who sits down and reads a Mexican newspaper for a while, then removes his sunglasses for a few seconds and puts them back on. It's Wayne!

All the agents: "Yes, it's him!"

Robinson: "Now let's see where he's going, where he's boarding, what plane he's getting on!"

All watch the screen as the video follows Wayne, who waits until the last minute to go into the boarding tunnel!

Ramos: "Shit, damn, fuck, that son of a bitch was heading to Cuba! Mother fuck!"

Robinson: "Can't we snatch him down there and get him out by boat?"

Ramos: "Maybe – but for now let's see where Wayne Boy is! I don't understand why flee over 10 years out in eight and a half and back with his family!"

Robinson: "The word is it wasn't going to be 10 years, it would be 25 to life per insiders at Judge McNamara's staff, leaked the info McNamara was going to hit Wayne with 25 to life! If Wayne got the same info, he might have thought his life was over and decided to flee!"

Ramos: "That theory might be true. There's a lot of gossip going on in the court. It's too late now, but check it out."

Robinson: "If he's in Cuba, can new have their police pick him up and ship him back?"

Ramos: "Not going to happen! The U.S. has no extradition

agreement with Cuba. We currently have 18 wanted guys down in Cuba that we can't touch! They never leave the island and have family and friends visit."

Robinson: "Shit, shit, shit, big mouth at the court! We fail to grab his [passport and now he's where we can't get him!"

Ramos: "I wonder how he could have put his plan together so quickly. Let's jam his brother, threaten him, scare the shit out of him and see if he sends any money to Wayne. He's losing his home to the bonding company, right?"

Robinson: "Well, not exactly. It's one of of four property homes he's bought, he'll lose maybe $80,000 but he's a multimillionaire with 52 doctors working under him – he's getting 25% of every hour they bill. Guy is really bringing in the bucks."

Ramos: "Let's scare him, doctors are generally pussies. Tell him if he sends one dollar to his brother, we'll shut his business down!"

Agent #1: "Can we do that?"

Ramos: "Naw! It's highly unlikely, but he won't know the difference. Do it in front of his wife, scare the hell out of her!"

Back in Cuba:

Wayne with 18 little kids, nine to 13 years old, has found a vacant lot with lots of junk, weeds, an old rusty wreck of a car.

The children, mostly boys (three girls) help clear the lot, rake it and take away the rocks. Wayne finds some pipes and begins building the back stop a neighbor come over with a roll of chicken wire. Tells Wayne take what he needs and to return the rest.

Four men come by, watch and offer to help remove the rusty car body. The men get a tractor, a chain, and drag the wreck away.

At the end of the day, the lot is fairly level. A crude back stop made of old pipes and chicken wire is complete! Tomorrow practice – Wayne now needs to see Chapo for gloves and equipment.

During the day, while the kids were in school, Wayne and Chapo ride together to the practice field. Wayne explains that the kids need shoes, socks, gloves, shirts, bats, balls, and bases.

Chapo says, "Let's tell my team mates."

At the field, Chapo calls a meeting and explains the situation and what Wayne and the kids need.

All his team mates are on board. All go to their lockers, get money and put the money into Chapo's cap.

Chapo hands Wayne his car keys, the cash and a paper giving an address of a man who sells shoes and gloves.

La Bamba, the all-star hitter and outfielder, offers to come with Wayne, who agrees. The two leave together. La Bamba's English is very limited and Wayne's Spanish is getting better. They figure it out.

Wayne has a pad of paper with outlines of each of the kids' feet with their names on the sheets. La Bamba drives to the little store. He negotiates with the manager, they agree on prices and a helper takes the kids' footprints to get the right size shoes.

The manager is so impressed, La Bamba is in his store, gets a camera and has his wife take their pictures. Then, tells her to please bring them lunch.

The three men walk through the store to a small patio courtyard with a large table and eight chairs. His wife scurried between the store patio and a small gate to the house they owned next door! Bringing plates of salami, cheeses, olives, chilies, pitchers of Cuban sweet tea, bread, and tortillas.

What a relaxed way to do business! Wayne opens his small cigar case and pulls out three cigars. The men light up! Excellent! So good! The helper comes and shows the men the samples of shoes. La Bamba picks a style for the kids.

One hour later, they have shoes, shirts, pants, and gloves.

La Bamba says, "I've got my camera, let's get some pictures with the kids and some of the team, this will be fun!"

When the kids get home from school, they gather at the lot awaiting Mr. Wayne and Chapo. Word has gotten out in the neighborhood that Chapo was coming and there are about 40 people sitting around the crude, dirt field.

Then, the team bus pulls up with nearly all the players. Wayne, La Bamba and Chapo have followed in Chapo's car. There is a photographer – the kids are so excited! They have been playing ball with a broomstick and an old tennis ball.

The team's manager, the grounds keeper, and five of his crew have followed in a big truck, followed by a flat bed truck with sod. Also on another flat bed is lumber.

The manager and the players gather the kids, call each of their names and gives each a cap, a shirt, a pair of ballplayer paints, socks, and a new pair of shoes.

Photos are taken and then the grounds crew prepares the soil with rakes, hoes, and shovels. Then all pitch in to roll out the fresh sod! A pitching mound is put together, then a real back stop is put up with high posts wire and on high up posts six solar lights.

The photographer follows each step of the way, snapping pictures.

Three bases are installed. Lines are marked just as it's getting dark. The solar spot lights come on, everyone cheers, a four inning ball game is put together with two players coaching the kids.

Wayne: "A fun time, Chapo?"

Chapo: "Reminds me of when I was a kid, this was a special day, Wayne!"

Wayne grins.

Wayne: "Let's burn a stogie, Chapo."

FBI rented house:

Robinson: "Ramos, guys, we have found Wayne Thomas in Havana."

All the agents gather around the large screen. On the screen was the front page of the Havana Star and a story about a Norte Americano helping a bunch of kids build a ball field.

There on the front page with the smiling, happy kids, Cuban ball player right in the middle was:

"Wayne Thomas"

Ramos: "Wayne Thomas, our fugitive building a ball field for Cuban kids!"

Ramos is livid.

"What the hell, who knows Spanish enough to read the rest of this' story?!"

Agent #1: "Ramos, aren't you Mexican? Don't you know Spanish writing?"

Ramos: "No, smart ass, I was born here and can talk Espanol a bit but not reading!"

Agent Sanchez: "I'll read the story."

All of the eight agents listen intently.

"Wayne, the American had noticed kids trying to play ball with a broomstick and an old tennis ball and decided to help!

Wayne called his friends, El Chapo and La Bamba to ask for their help.

The whole team pitched in to help the kids fix up a vacant lot into a small ball field, buy the kids uniforms and equipment!"

There are pictures of players helping roll out the sod and kids with new equipment.

Ramos: "Let's get our men down there to snatch him."

Robinson: "That might not be very popular in Havana."

Robinson smiles.

Ramos: "screw Cuba,screw Havana, they're a bunch of damn' commies! Set up the snatch!"

Robinson stares at Ramos, he can't believe what he's hearing.

The next morning, Wayne hears the sounds of hammers and quickly gets a pair of shorts on, throws on a t-shirt, slips into some flip-flops and heads toward the noise.

It's 7:30 AM. The ballpark crew are back and with some carpenters who are building two small bleachers for the fans.

The ground crews have brought a large fiberglass water tank and two new lawnmowers, donated by the stadium

The photographers snap pictures of the follow up story in the Havana Star.

Wayne is interviewed and thinks, "What the hell is the difference, after the front page picture and story!"

The following day is more pictures on the building of the bleachers, pictures of Wayne and his interview.

By 3:00 PM., the bleachers are finished, grass has been watered, lines are freshened and the kids began to arrive.

Wayne: "Kids, to be better ball players, you must first practice. Then after a couple hours, everyone goes home. Eat and do your homework."

The kids protest, "Don't have homework! Our parents are bringing food about 6:00 PM. and some for you, Mr. Wayne!"

Wayne doubts the homework story, but since the kids want to play he agrees to a three inning scrimmage.

The kids cheer. They are so excited. Sure enough, parents and other neighbors bring buckets of food, cups of rice, beans and iced tea are eaten in the new bleachers.

Chapo, La Bamba, and four other players show up just as the solar flood lights come on! The kids cheer once again.

Wayne is sitting with Chapo, watching La Bamba play with the kids.

Wayne: "Wow, this reminds me of when my two kids were small, so much fun! Look at how happy those kids are!"

Chapo: "I'm looking at how happy you are, Wayne!"

The kid scrimmage for three very awkward innings, tons of mistakes.

Wayne blows his whistle.

Wayne: "That's it, kids! Enough for tonight! Do your homework!"

In broken Spanish, Wayne thanks the parents for the food and drinks.

Chapo walks out to the street and talks with about 10 men that Wayne thinks are fans.

Chapo walks back to Wayne and smiles.

Chapo: "Those guys want to meet you and talk."

Wayne: "What about, Chapo?"

Chapo smiles.

Chapo: "They want a ball park for their kids and have found a field the owner will donate for the kids.

Wayne grins.

Wayne: "Chapo, what have we got ourselves into? Sure, we'll talk but NO promises!"

Chapo waves the parents to come over.

The men come and sit in the stands. One takes charge and begins speaking very clear English.

"Our children have no place close to play. They love baseball and play under a street light playing stick-ball."

Wayne gets the address of the proposed future ballpark. Chapo knows the area and will make a map and directions for Wayne to find the site tomorrow.

All the men are very excited and act as if the ballpark was moving forward.

At 9:00 the next morning after dropping off Chapo at the ball field, Wayne follows the map and wanders a bit and finds the empty field of about three acres.

Two of the parents were waiting for Wayne. The three men walk the field – not too bad – but will have to have a bulldozer grade the field level.

The men introduce Wayne to the landowner, a kind man who

saw the story in the paper and wanted to help the children around their neighborhood.

He will give the land to the kids if they will build a small ball park for the ninos.

The team photographer shows up with his camera and video camera.

Wayne introduces each father and the landowner.

He asks Carlos if he's going to run the pictures of this site.

Carlos: "Not without a story, Wayne."

Wayne: "Whew, we are starting to load my plate pretty fast here, but I want to help."

Carlos: "Wayne, I'll try to hold the story and the pictures for two or three days – what is your plan for this field?"

Wayne: "Need a bulldozer with a laser level for about two days. The field slopes down too much, needs to be perfectly level! *Then* we can do a proper plan."

Carlos: "I'll ask around, Wayne."

Two days later in morning Havana Star:

Wayne's picture with the two fathers looking at an empty field appeared in the third page of the Havana Star and the papers' artist had made an art drawing of what she thought the new ball field would look like, along with a before and after of the first project!

Again, there was Wayne's picture, along with Chapo's, tossing balls with the kids. Wayne was hitting shag balls for the kids.

A picture of La Bamba hitting some shag balls for the kids!

"A real nice tear jerker story!", thinks Wayne.

Chapo is by the pool in a bathrobe, reading the morning Havana Star.

Chapo: "Hey Wayne, good morning Mr. Sleepy Senor."

Wayne mumbles, "Buenos dias, Chapo."

Chapo picks up an unlit cigar, puts it close to his mouth and does a decent Grocho Marx impression wiggling his eyebrows and says, "Well this is another fine mess you got us into, Senor Wayne."

Wayne laughs and does a spit-ta.

Chapo: "How'd you do that?"

Wayne takes a sip of water and does another spit-ta.

Both men smile and both read the paper again. Chapo helps with the reading then slaps his forehead. There on the table is an English version of the Havana Star – he hands it to Wayne.

The maid and the cook bring a small tray with their breakfasts. Both men's plates are covered with pan lids to keep the dishes warm, also a pot of fresh coffee, bowl of chopped fruit, and a flat bowl of hot tortillas.

Chapo: "First, we swim then we talk, okay?"

The men discuss the project after a 10 minute swim.

The cook has brought over a heater plate to warm up the breakfast.

Chapo: "George, you take good care of me."

George the Cook: "Yes, I know Mr. Chapo. No young ladies this week? You want I make a special drink with three blue pills!"

George smiles.

"Eh?"

Chapo smiles back.

Chapo: "I'll let you know, George. Thanks for your concern over my sex life?"

George grins and says, "When you are ready, Chapo."

Wayne: "Chapo is eating a black beans and rice dish, scooping it with folded tortilla with some pesto, made with black beans, corn, and chili sauce that was so perfect, he could eat it for breakfast every day! A single egg has been cooked perfectly on top of the rice and beans.

Full, they lit cigars and read the story again. Chapo's phone rings, it's one of the players. Chapo puts on speaker phone and sets the phone on the poolside table, then asks the player to repeat.

His uncle has seen the recent story on page three and wants to help – he grades the road and has the level. The uncle will work for free, he just needs some gas money and a helper that knows how to use survey equipment.

Wayne worked one summer on a survey crew.

Wayne: "Tell him I'll run the survey equipment and buy the gas. Ask him what time Saturday morning."

Chapo: "Says 7:00 – 8:00 AM, okay?"

Wayne:" 8:00 AM will be good and thank you so much, muchas gracias!"

It was Wednesday morning and the team was playing at home Friday and Sunday afternoon at 1:30. Chapo has gotten Wayne special box seats for Sunday – he was pitching as reliever Friday for the last two innings.

He would help with building the new field on Saturday, how nice was that!

Thursday, Wayne went alone on Chapo's Vespa scooter to the new site. Soon, he was standing with four men who were asking a lot of questions in Spanish that Wayne couldn't understand much of what was said.

A 10 year old kid with excellent English became a translator, he has a copy of the English version of the Havana Star showing the proposed site. That's why the men were there with rakes, hoes, shovels, ready to work with bandannas on their heads.

Wayne almost told them wait till Saturday, but he didn't want to dampen their enthusiasm. He pointed out weeds to be chopped. Large rocks to be set off to the side.

Wayne: "I'll be back in three hours, OK?

The Fathers: "Si, si, we are OK."

Wayne drives through crazy Havana traffic nearly getting hit by a car, gets to the stadium stopped by security.

Wayne: "Please tell Chapo or La Bamba that Mr. Wayne needs to see one of them."

Security Guard: "Sure, you know them?"

Wayne: "Yes."

Security Guard: "OK, please come in."

Wayne greets La Bamba.

Wayne: "Hey, my friend."

La Bamba: "Hey Wayne."

Wayne: "I've got a dozer for Saturday and Sunday for the new field. Should be able to work longer hours if we had some solar post lights on small telephone poles."

La Bamba: "I'll see our field groundskeeper, he found the lights for our first little field. Let's see if he can find some more!"

FBI rented house:

The house now has a big screen connected to their computer.

Robinson: "Hey Ramos, come in here and take a look!"

Ramos is in sweats, running shoes and a hoodie.

Agent: "Ramos, you look like our fugitive in Mexico City."

The other agents laugh along with Agent Robinson.

Robinson grins.

Robinson: "You're going to enjoy this story from yesterday's Havana Star, page three."

Robinson cues up the pictures of the men with Wayne looking at the empty field.

The next picture is an art drawing of another completed ball diamond.

Ramos is getting pissed.

Ramos: "So what, some more pictures of our escapee and his damn' kiddie ball field?"

Robinson: "No, he's building a second field construction, begins this weekend."

All the agents are smiling, a couple laughing.

Ramos: "You knuckleheads let him get away and now he's shoving it in our face and you shitheads are laughing about this second ball field, was probably paid for out of the money he stole!"

Robinson: "Uh boss, I don't believe he stole any money."

Ramos is livid now.

Ramos: "He was convicted, convicted, remember?! And by the way Robinson, have you jammed Wayne's doctor brother and the doctor's wife yet?"

Robinson: "No, not yet."

Ramos: "Go do it *now*, take shit-for-brains Mr. Havana Star with you. Give me a video copy when you get back and the good doctor better look real scared and his wife better look like she wet her pants."

Both men leave and head for Wayne's brother.

FBI rented house in Jefferson County:

Dr. Les Thomas works mostly from home with a large office with video players so he can speak and talk to his contract doctors in person via video.

The agents walk to the door.

Robinson: "You handle the rough talk, I'll just look mean and glare, OK?!"

After the agents show their badges, they also decline coffee.

Agent: "Dr. Thomas, we need to speak to you about your brother with you and your wife!"

Dr. Les Thomas: "Why my wife? Why not just me?"

Agent, bluffing: "Get your wife, doc or we'll have to take you both to the station for this interview!"

Dr. Les Thomas is getting irritated.

Dr. Les Thomas: "I'll get her."

Les brings Cheryl into his office with the agents.

Dr. Les Thomas: "If this is about my brother-"

The agent held up his hand for Les to stop.

Agent: "Shut up and listen. Your brother Wayne skipped bail and is in Cuba – if you aided him in any way, *any way*, the FBI will shut down this crappy little rent-a-quack scam you got going in a non-retail building. And when you both are in jail, who's going to care for the little ones?"

Cheryl begins crying, Les is getting angry, how dare they talk to his wife and he in that manner, in their own house!

Agent: "If we find out you are sending any funds to Cuba, we'll have your ass and seize your assets. Americans are prohibited from any financial dealing with Cuba or traveling to Cuba.

Try that shit and your kids could be wards of the county. Wayne already screwed you out of one of your homes when he skipped – you must be pretty pissed off at him right now?"

Dr. Les Thomas: "Not as pissed as I am over you two goons, coming into my home and acting like animals, threatening my wife and I with a bullshit threat. I'll tell you what, give your boss a message, OK, OK?"

Agent: "OK!"

Dr. Les Thomas: "Tell him Wayne's brother is proud of his brother and of all the people he's helped save their homes from foreclosure and good for him building ball fields in Cuba. He's a decent man, something you low lives wouldn't understand! Gentlemen, please leave."

Robinson is walking out of the driveway.

Robinson: "Well that went nicely!" he smiles

Inside Dr. Les Thomas's house, Les is looking at the agents walking down the drive.

Dr. Les Thomas: "Damn' pricks!"

Cheryl: "What are we going to do, Les? We can't help Wayne without getting trouble. You heard those agents, we have already lost a house."

Dr. Les Thomas: "Those two goons came here to scare us into not helping Wayne or Sarah – well screw them! Cheryl, I've got something to show you."

Les opens his desk and hands Cheryl a copy of the Havana Star (in English).

Cheryl: "Oh my god, is that Wayne?"

Les proudly grins.

Dr. Les Thomas: "Yep, it's your brother in law and my baby brother."

Cheryl sits down, stunned and reads the story.

Cheryl: "Wow! Wayne can't have been in Cuba but a few days! Why isn't he in hiding? How did he get down there? The bonding company is threatening to take one of our houses!"

Dr. Les Thomas: "Cheryl, listen, the house is gone we have four more homes. We are clearing over $150,000 per month.

Wayne and Sarah, Chad and Billy need our help now! Those FBI goons made me realize something! *Family is important*, and we haven't helped our family enough."

Cheryl: "But we put up title of a house that we are losing $100,000, isn't that enough?!"

Dr. Les Thomas: "Family is family, Cheryl. No, I don't feel it's enough! Sarah is working 50 hours a week, both Chad and Billy are working part time jobs and playing baseball. I want to help more and I want you to be with me on this. I don't want to sneak around with giving funds to my family!"

Cheryl: "Are you sure we won't get in trouble?"

Dr. Les Thomas: "No problem."

He hands money to Sarah. The boys have to be a little more careful giving Wayne some cash.

Cheryl: "How could we? Those FBI agents sounded so very nasty!"

Dr. Les Thomas: "They came into our house to scare us, Cheryl! Are you scared?"

Cheryl: "I was! Now I'm mad! So very mad!"

Dr. Les Thomas: "Good, me too! Are we a team?"

Cheryl: "Yes, we're a team my love!"

Dr. Les Thomas: "Good, good. Now here's the plan. You go to the Walmart, buy us five phones – burner phones with say 500 minutes, then see Sarah and give her this amount of money."

Les hands Sarah a piece of paper with $30,000 on it!

Dr. Les Thomas: "Draw it out of four of our personal accounts. Never going above $10,000 because the feds are notified on anything over $10,000."

Cheryl: "I'll have it done today, Les. I'll leave after I feed the little ones (a five-year-old boy and a three-year-old girl)."

Later at Sarah's work (a large furniture store):

Cheryl waits for a half hour for Sarah to wait on her. The two women walk through the store.

Sarah: "What furniture are you interested in, Cheryl?"

Cheryl pots a large dining room table and chairs, and points to the table. Both sit down.

The store sales manager walks past and smiles.

Cheryl slides over the front page of the Havana Star.

Cheryl: "Sarah, have you seen this?!"

Sarah: "No I haven't, I knew he was in Cuba but I thought was in hiding! Not on the friggin' front page!"

Sarah smiles.

"Good picture, huh? Looks so happy with those kids."

Cheryl: "Sarah, it's a great story! Keep the paper. Show the boys what their dad is up to!"

Cheryl: "Les and I want you and the boys to know family is so very important to us and we apologize for not helping more!"

Sarah: "The bond was wonderful – it kept Wayne out of jail! So sorry you are going to lose the house."

Cheryl: "Les has a plan! We have five burner phones."

Cheryl hands Sarah a paper with the new numbers.

"We only talk on the throw-away phones, OK? Les wants you and at least one of the boys to go to Miami, then to the Bahamas."

Sarah: "But. but we don't have the time or money."

Cheryl holds up her hand.

Cheryl: "Find the time and call in sick! As far as money-"

She slides a package.

"Don't worry!"

Sarah takes a quick peek – there are a lot of hundred dollar bills.

Cheryl: "There is $38,000 in there. When you get down to Cuba, give Wayne $10,000 and let him know we love him and we will send more money and not to worry! Go to the Smoke Zone conference room, talk to Wayne's friend Zack on instructions on how to get into Cuba through the Bahamas!"

Sarah begins crying.

Sarah: "Thank you so much, Cheryl!"

Cheryl: "Now, now, Sarah. Suck it up, your manager is starting to watch you now!"

Sarah: "Good, I'll tell him I've gotten sick and have to go home. Billy is home from college for eight days. I'll see if he's ready for an adventure!"

Sarah smiles.

The women hug, and Sarah goes to her boss. She's very sick, she says.

Sarah calls Billy.

Sarah: "Stay home we need to talk and only on the special phones."

Sarah goes to the Smoke Zone, sees Zack, shows him the story and he smiles.

Zack: "When are you going, Sarah?"

Sarah: "Tomorrow!"

Zack: "Good, here's how you get in."

He explains the no stamp of the passport drill! Sarah gets it.

Zack: "Also Sarah, when you see Wayne, give him this Cuban contact, Mr. Soto of Primo Cigar. He could possibly help with funding of ball fields for kids! Could I make a photo copy of the newspaper story for the guys? They will love it!"

Sarah thinks, "Why not? The feds know he's there!"

"Sure Zack, make all you want – give me back one."

Sarah goes to talk with Billy.

Back in Havana, Cuba:

Saturday morning, Wayne is at the new site at 7:00 with gas cans, rakes, hoes, shovels.

The bulldozer and the men are already there, ready to go. There is still a morning fog. A Jose introduces a Miguel and a Roberto, who has an ancient survey tri-pod.

Wayne has never seen such an old instrument!

Roberto grins.

Roberto: "1933. Still works fine, amigo!"

For the next day and a half, a lot of progress La Bamba has had eight solar spot lights delivered and the lights provide light enough so they work until 9:00 PM.

By 11:00 AM., the field is level and they all hug and have lunch together, have a rum drink. A team photographer takes pictures of the men, the field, the dozer, Wayne at the survey equipment.

Wayne goes to his small house, showers, cleans up, and goes to La Bamba's large closet. He picks out a white Cuban shirt, a white pair of pants, and a pair of sandals.

Wayne: "Cool."

Wayne heads for the stadium.

At the stadium, Wayne is early. The game is at 2:00 PM. - it's only one – and hands the usher his ticket. They go to the box seating, 12 seats. Surprise, Mr. Soto of Primo Cigars is there along with a famous man! It's Raul Castro, El Presidente of Cuba! Mr. Soto hugs Wayne, introduces Raul Castro to Wayne Thomas. Photos are taken by three photographers.

The men smile, relax, Raul and Soto out of courtesy to Wayne speak English. Castro has been following the story of the kids' ball fields.

Castro: "How's the second field coming?"

Wayne tells the men the field is now level as of 11:00 AM. Somehow Raul Castro knows this already. Both men offer to help any way they can on the second field. Castro knows the first field needs more stands, people are standing around! He will see it gets done!

Wayne is quite happy! What a fine sunny Havana day!

Wayne tries to stay awake but he nods off. Soto and Raul smile and let him doze a little. A few minutes later, Wayne wakes up in a haze, he is dreaming in front of him is Sarah and his son Billy.

Big smiles from the wife and son.

Sarah: "Hello, sleepyhead!"

Wayne introduces his wife and son to Mr. Soto and President Castro.

Another round of hugs and photos.

Chapo, La Bamba and the rest of the team come by to shake hands with Wayne, Mr. Soto, and the President, Castro.

Even more photos.

It's so good to be with wife and son on such a beautiful day!

Turned out Zack of the Smoke Zone had called Mr. Soto and arranged for Sarah and Billy to be picked up at the airport that morning (by Mike)!

Mike informed Sarah and Billy what Wayne had been doing, where Wayne was living, what he was doing with the kids and the ball fields.

The game ended, home team lost eight to six. Oh well, it was a beautiful day, beautiful day. Good bye hugs follow. Raul Castro hands Wayne his card.

Castro: "Call me, my amigo."

Billy wanted to meet the Cuban players, especially La Bamba.

Mike: "Sure, follow me."

Billy is introduced to the players, who sign lots of autographs.

The Cuban players asks, "Does this 6'5" Billy play ball?"

"Yes, he's a pitcher but more of a hitter!"

"Let's see! Come on, take a few swings at the bat."

Billy grins.

Billy: "Sure!"

He takes of his windbreaker and shirt down to the t-shirt.

Assistant Coach: "Wow, check this kid out!"

The second pitch went over the fence, 430 feet, oh wow! All the Cuban players laugh and clap each other on the back.

"More Billy, more!"

All the players trot onto the field to their regular positions.

A top pitcher takes the mound, prepared to strike out Billy. What's going on?

About 2,000 sit and watch out of curiosity.

Strike one, ball one, BAM, another along ball gone over the left field fence!

Billy, smiling broadly trots around the bases. All the players come trotting in, ribbing the pitcher, who smiles good naturally.

The teams' manager has just watched this beautiful, blonde giant hit two home runs, one of them an easy peasy lob, but the second a real hard, fast ball by his second best starter!   Wow!

Manager Roberto Luna comes by to talk with Billy. He has excellent English and had played in the U.S. for three years for the Cubs.

Roberto pulls Billy off to one side – away from the others.

Roberto: "Sit, please. Billy, what are you doing with your baseball? College? Schools? How do you feel about your dad being down here?"

Soto: "Here's the deal, Billy; you want to play in the majors some day, right?

We lost our game today because of not enough offense in our lineup. La Bamba, our best hitter often gets walks. I need some firepower behind La Bamba. It doesn't pay much, but you could see a lot of your dad help him with the kids, eat wonderful Cuban food, and enjoy our music!

Do you like to dance? Eh?"

Soto smiles.

"Dance the salsa? No? Well you can learn the dance surfer

dude – if you can really, really hit in two years, we will have major scouts down here drooling over you! In the meantime, you can help us win the Caribbean championship! Want a real try out in one to two days, slugger?"

Billy: "Can we get together tomorrow, Mr. Luna?"

Luna: "Sure, no problem Billy. I'll see you in one or two days. Oh, and another thing, we have beautiful beaches, beautiful Swedish visitors and our Latin women are the most beautiful in the world!"

Wayne, Sarah, Billy, Mr. Roberto, Luna, and the team's manager, Soto insists on paying for all the food and drinks.

Monday, Wayne takes the day off to be with Sarah and Billy. Chapo has given Sarah and Wayne his house to spend the night Chapo and Billy spend the night in the guest house.

Tuesday, Wane and Billy visit kid's park number two. Wayne is amazed the backstop is up and the stands are nearly completed. The field has been graded down fine, ready for sod. One of the workers said, "Mr. Soto and El Presidente had come by the field and said the field would have a sprinkler system.

Sarah is shopping with a nice young woman from El Primo Cigar Company.

Two days later, at the FBI HQ in Denver, Colorado:

Robinson: "Well Ramos, our boy Wayne made the front page again. No, page three this time."

Ramos: "Another damn' kiddie ball field?"

Robinson: "Nope, he's attending a ball game with El Presidente,

Raul Castro, his wife Sarah, son Billy, and a big cigar company big shot, a Mr. Soto."

Robinson shows Ramos the photo. Ramos is furious!

Ramos: "Speed up the plan to snatch Wayne Thomas!"

Ramos: "This Mr. Wayne Thomas is convicted, not sentenced. Some big mouth, loose lips let it slip that the judge is giving Wayne a pretty harsh sentence and he flees. We look like jerks with our dicks in our hands! No one sees to it that he surrendered his passport! Now! Now! Now! His face is on the front page of some commie newspaper three times – set up the snatch on Thomas. I'm sick of being made to look foolish!"

Cuba Gran Stadium, Havana:

On Wednesday, Billy Thomas went to the Gran Stadium to try out for the Havana Team. The players greeted Billy warmly, remembering his hitting two long balls during the drill.

Billy hits in the batting cage. The hitting coach likes what he sees. A sweet swing, good timing, quick bat.

Coach Rios: "Billy, OK enough of the cage. Let's have you step up to the plate."

Billy moves to the batter's box.

Coach Rios: "Hey, let's have two relievers (pitchers) throw some pitches for Senior Billy."

1st Pitcher: "How hard do you want me to throw?"

Coach Rios: "Start slow for three to four pitches, then bring the heat; all you have!"

Catcher says to Billy, "Watch this guy. He will start slow then give you a curve ball, then a sinker, then some real heat, 94 – 98. Hit it, kid!"

The pitcher warms up with the catcher – six pitches – then he's ready!

Second pitch to Billy, pow! Long hit, just foul.

Third pitch a hit! Dropping in center field! The right fielder can't get to it!

Coach Rios: "That's a single! Billy, OK you are now the second batter."

Billy hits the sinker for another hit just over the head of the second baseman.

Coach Rios calls loudly, "Double Billy, man on second and third gives the signal to the pitch bring the heat!"

Billy waits on the fast ball lets it go by and thinks, "OK, if that's what he's going to throw I'll be ready!" He digs his cleats in!

Next pitch, pow! A home run!

Coach Rios, to his assistant, "How fast?"

Coach Rios is holding a speed gun.

Coach Rios: "96 MPH!"

Rios has seen enough. He feels he has the hitter to back up La Bamba.

Coach Rios: "OK Billy, enough hitting – your positions you like?"

Billy: "First base and right field!"

Coach Rios: "OK, here's the deal Billy; we're putting you in right field for three innings. That will be it! Game's at 4:30! Let's have some fun Billy – baseball is a fun game right?!"

Billy smiles.

Billy: "Yeah Mr. Rios, baseball's a lot of fun!"

Billy thinks, "Yeah when I can get hits!"

Rios gathers the team.

Coach Rios: "This is Billy, he's from Denver. He's playing with us for a little while today in right field."

Game at 4:30:

A 6'5" pitcher, Pedro Gonzales shares an extra uniform with Billy. Billy thanks Pedro.

Gonzales: "No problem, Billy! Hope you do good, Amigo."

Billy is amazed, there must be 20,000 people in the stands. He looks up and sees his mom and dad sitting in some great seats, they don't see him!

Cuban National Anthem! Loud cheers follow.

"Let's play ball (in Spanish)!"

The other team gets one walk, one hit driving the man on base to third stays on first. Chapo strikes out the next two batters. Next batter flies toward Billy, he speeds up and catches the fly ball – inning over!

One hit gets to first – one strikes out, man on first steals second! Wow, real speed!

La Bamba is walked – goes to first!

Billy is up at bat – teammate Pedro Gonzales has told Billy the pitcher he will be facing throws strikes 90% of the time on the first pitch.

La Bamba: "Don't be afraid to let it rip, Billy."

First pitch a little fat in the strike zone, pow! Billy hits a triple standing up. Billy is waved off from the third base coach to not try for home. La Bamba and the other teammate score! Crowd goes wild, loud cheers!

3ʳᵈ Base Coach: "Way to go, Billy."

Coach Rios is smiling. He likes what he sees happening once opponent coaches realize that Billy can hit, they will think twice walking La Bamba.

Nice long fly ball in right field. Billy tags up and races to home. Another run scores! Three to zero.

In the third inning with two outs, La Bamba is again walked – goes to first – and the crowd boos! Two strikes, two balls, pitcher throwing some junk. Billy gets an inside slider, bang! Home run! Billy trots around the bases and is greeted by the smiling La Bamba and the whole team who clap Billy on the back – huge cheers from the fans. Billy looks up, his dad and mom are hugging and laughing!

Coach Rios: "Hey Billy, come here my big little friend! Way to go, nice hitting! Remember I said I would play you only the first three innings?"

Billy: "Yeah Coach Rios, I understand that's cool!"

Coach Rios: "But good job Billy, way to go."

Head Coach: "Rios, the crowd is going to really give us hell today when we pull Billy and the Havana Star will want to know what the hell! Why pull the Norte Americano?"

Coach Rios grins.

Coach Rios: "Yeah, I love it."

Rios is a seasoned pro and knows he has really gotten something he's been needing for a long time; two real hitters behind La Bamba.

The photographer from the Havana Star after getting some excellent photos of Billy's hits, celebrations with teammates he now has photos of Billy's proud mom and dad smiling and hugging. This will be some story in tomorrow's paper – hold the presses!

Raul Castro and two other men have joined Wayne and Sarah in their box with Senor Soto of El Primo Cigar.

All pump the parents' hands.

Castro addresses Wayne and Sarah.

Castro: "Congratulations! Your son has a sweet swing. I'm sure my brother's family is watching right now on their TV."

Game ends, six to three. Havana wins!!

Photographers are all over Billy and want La Bamba and him to pose together in several poses.

The team after showers, change of clothes, goes to a large cantina to celebrate. They are joined by the coaches and Billy's proud parents. After about an hour, the celebration ends. Billy and his parents go two doors down the street to a smaller more private restaurant.

Sarah: "Wayne, it looks like Cuba is going to be your home for the rest of your life and it's been a few years since I've seen you so happy!"

Wayne: "But I really, really miss you and Chad and the dogs! And our life together!"

Sarah: "Wayne, you did the only thing to survive. That terrible judge, those awful FBI goons."

Wayne: "Thank you so much, my dear. Love you, babe."

They kiss. Billy smiles.

Sarah looks at Billy.

Sarah: "So, Mr. Big Shot hitter, have you decided for the Havana Team?

Billy: "Mom, today was like the cherry on the best cake

you could ever eat! It's like what I've been trained for and it's graduation day!"

Sarah: "Weren't you nervous?"

Billy: "Mom, it was *amazing*! The huge crowd didn't make me nervous, it gave me energy and concentration I've never felt before! It seemed so natural! In college, the number of fans would may be 80 – 100 tops. I got hyped up and a charge out of the cheers of 22,000, and the music! I love Cuban music! This has to be one of the best days of my life! What wonderful warm people!"

Wayne: "The Havana general manager was asking you a strange question, if you had a surfboard? What's that about? Does he want to go surfing with you?"

Billy: "I was asked the same question! It seems like the team's publicity department want me to pose with my surf board."

Billy laughs.

"Wouldn't care if I had struck out today. I have to go back to the stadium in a little bit and if it doesn't take too long, let's eat at the beach!"

Wayne smiles.

Wayne: "I'm sure you and your mom will like the beach, the clear blue water and the incredibly friendly people."

Back at the stadium:

At the stadium, Coach Rios was with the photographers and a small group of people.

Coach Rios waves Billy to come over.

Coach Rios: "Hey Billy, come here!"

One of the men comes over with a surfboard.

Coach Rios points to the men with the board.

Coach Rios: "Jose, here is a surfboard artist, he will create a design on a surfboard for you!"

Billy: "That's very nice coach, but can I ask without being rude why the surfboard? Why at a baseball stadium?"

Coach Rios: "Sorry Billy, I didn't explain, excuse me! The team's publicity department have a big push to give attention to the team's new Colorado slugger!"

Billy: "Slugger, Coach Rios? Aren't we rushing things calling me a slugger after three innings and two at bats?"

Coach Rios grins and shrugs.

Coach Rios: "Billy, what's your batting average? Right now! Right now!"

They both laugh.

Billy poses with the surfboard in uniform and with the surfboard artist.

After 20 minutes, Chapo, La Bamba, Billy and his folks head for the beach a few minutes away.

At the beach:

The group in swimsuits are surrounded by baseball fans. Chapo and La Bamba sign autographs. Some of the fans were at the game earlier and want Billy's signature.

Chapo: "Get used to it, Billy."

La Bamba: "Si, as long as he keeps on hitting!"

Wayne and Sarah get plates of delicious snacks and some rum drinks. After a few bites, the guys realized the crowd wasn't going away and changed plans. Wayne called on his phone.

Chapo: "Hey guys, Mr. Soto wants us to join him for dinner! Si? Everyone agrees by nodding yes.

At the restaurant:

The dinner party has grown to over twenty and includes Raul Castro. Photos are taken and the photographers then leave. Everyone relaxes. Raul Castro has choppy English and reverts back to Spanish.

A very tasty meal – a bit different from Denver Mexican food, but the Thomas family likes it a lot!

Next morning in the Havana Star, Billy is on the front page! Colorado surfer dude hitter – a brief story on Billy, pictures of both hits and the home run. Billy is in full swing hitting the ball. There's a celebration picture at home plate getting mobbed by the team.

There's also a photo of Billy with a surfboard – new art has been photoshopped onto the board billy was holding.

Unknown to Billy, the artist had worked through the night to finish the board.

The board was delivered to Chapo's house to be given to Billy. It had a picture of Billy with long, blonde hair hitting a ball – in vivid colors! The board was truly a fine piece of art!

One day off and the deal on Billy's small salary was worked out a one year contract.

Back at the FBI house:

Robinson is trying not to smile, he hands Ramos a copy of the Havana Star, English edition.

Ramos: "Some more of the commie rag! Shit, shit, fuck! Damn!"

Ramos reads every word.

Robinson looks at a second copy.

Robinson: "Billy Thomas looks good, eh boss?"

Robinson tries to keep a straight face.

Ramos: "Surfer dude? What's surfing got to do with a baseball? Dumb fucking commies! What's up with the snatch plan to get Wayne Thomas?"

Robinson: "Not a good time right now, lot's of good press on the son, the new ball fields for little kids by Wayne Thomas – The Brass wants us to wait!"

Ramos: "Mother- shit, shit, damn!"

At the Havana Airport:

Wayne and Billy say good bye to Sarah.

Wayne: "Have a good flight, my love. It was so special having you here. Keep the money my brother and sister gave you. Billy and I are OK. He got the big contract."

Wayne laughs.

Sarah: "$2,500 a month is enough?"

Wayne: "Here, a family can live well on $500 per month! I mean *real* well! And save a lot!"

Sarah: "Here."

Sarah hands her husband $3,000.

"Before coming here, your brother gave me this to give to you! He and your sister said they would help and give us $5,000 per month each."

Wayne smiles.

Wayne: "Well, well! What a pleasant surprise! I thought money was Les's god sister and her husband bought a new home in Pasadena and said the first $5,000 they gave us would be all the y could do! Wonder why the change of heart?"

Sarah: "Well, Les said the FBI tried to intimidate him and it really pissed him off! He called your defense attorney and told them what had happened with the FBI threats were made. Are the threats true at all? No, it was just cheap, nothing. Threats meant to scare Les and his wife, Amy. He was quite angry and called your sister. Anyway, they said our family will receive $10,000 per month. I think he's good for it!"

Wayne: "Should be! Makes 1.2 million per year! And my sister and her husband make almost a mil."

Sarah: "I meant really committed to doing the cash each month! Anyway, seems your family has decided to circle the wagons!"

Wayne: "How soon can Chad visit? Billy needs his old fielder's glove!"

Sarah: "In three weeks, and he's coming with Zack and the Smoke Zone guys. I'll mail Billy's glove."

Wayne gives Sarah one of Mr. Soto's Primo Cigar cards. Mail it here! Attention: Surfer Dude!

They share laughs.

Sarah: "Chad has seven months left on the last year of his scholarship. So that's not an immediate money worry. Didn't want to worry you but Chad is having his throwing arm checked out!

He might have to have Tommy John surgery! I'll let you know by calling Mr. Soto!"

Sarah hugs her two guys.

Billy: "Mom, tell Chad how great the music is here!"

Sarah: "He can hear it himself soon!"

At the FBI rented house:

Ramos: "Robinson, what's the plan for snatching 'El baseball Senor Wayne'?"

Robinson: "The plan was to have three of our Cuban agents grab Wayne Thomas, inject him, take him one and a half hours North to a small fishing harbor where a fast boat will take him to Miami. The boat's expensive!"

Ramos: "How expensive?"

Robinson: "$400,000 cash!"

Ramos: "Why so much? Never mind, we will pay it when everything is set!"

Robinson: "Boss, I thought the snatch was on hold for a while and if it is, we'll never get the $400,000 to pay for the fast boat!"

Ramos: "I've got the $400,000 right now!"

Robinson: "I keep the financial books for our group, we have a little over $90,000. Where's the rest to come from?"

Ramos: "Robinson, you forget we seized $176,000 in Wayne Thomas's accounts and another $256,000 in seized North American Law funds! Combined over $400,000, presto, money problem solved!"

Robinson: "Can we legally use the money to snatch Thomas?"

Ramos: "All the defendants charged were convicted, including Thomas. All are in jail except Thomas. Using convicted felons funds to capture the one who fled! The upper brass will bitch but if we get Thomas, they'll shut up!"

Robinson: "What about orders to stand down on the snatch until the Havana Star quits doing stories about Thomas and his kid, Billy? Too much good will be in the press and the U.S. is trying to do some sort of a small normalization with Cuba! A snatch could screw up an agreement! Cubans love their baseball."

Ramos: "You think Cuba is going to care that much about one man and his kid? Don't think so."

Robinson: "It better go very smooth, or we will all be in trouble!"

Ramos: "They're pros, and once Thomas is back in jail in Miami, he's ours! And the state department who wants to play kissy face with the Castro's can kiss my ass! They can yell and protest but we'll have Thomas and they can't wind that back even if it pisses off a bunch of Cuban baseball fans!"

Havana National Stadium home game:

Warm up, stretches, Billy has a new uniform and the new hot surf board is leaning by the dugout! He smiles and shakes his head.

Billy: "Oh well!"

Lots of photographers and writers, some from Miami, another from U.S.A. Today, Wall Street Journal, N.Y. Times, Denver Post and of course, the Havana Star!

The Cuban National Anthem comes on!

Umpire, in Spanish: "Let's play ball!"

Larger crowd than Billy's first game. He would be batter number four and La Bamba number three.

The Havana Team would bat bottom of an inning.

Chapo starts as pitcher and strikes out the first two batters. The third hitter hits a nice stand up double. The next batter hits a pop up inning half over!

Havana at bat – Rios gives his hitters some tips on the pitcher they're facing.

Throws a lot of heat first two pitches. First pitch in strike zone, second pitch just outside, and the third pitch a big wind up, then drops down to a 68 MPH sinker!

First batter let's the first pitch go by – strike! Second pitch, battery swings – strike two out of strike zone! Third pitch slowly drops in – strike three!

The second batter is patient and gets a walk, goes to first.

Next up, La Bamba! Music plays. Richie Valen's La Bamba! The crowd goes wild!

The pitcher walks La Bamba – crowd boos!

Billy is up, but before getting into the batter's box, Billy trots over and pats his surfboard for luck (as per Coach Rios).

Music blares an old Beach Boy tune, 'Surfin' Safari'! The crowd sings along, almost all the fans know the song's words.

Billy smiles to the fans and tips his cap. He walks to the batter's box and digs in. The fans grow quiet.

Here comes the fastball in the strike zone – crack! The bat splits !the ball drops in deep center field. Billy's hit drives in a teammate on second and La Bamba who slides into home! Billy runs to second.

Beach Boy music continues! Another song plays.

Billy does a little two step while on the bag at second base, music starts again. The crowd laughs.

The pitcher turns around to see what's going on behind him on second. Billy tips his cap, taunting the pitcher.

The pitcher can't concentrate and begins throwing balls, throws a wild pitch, the catcher can't reach the ball and it goes to the very back of the backstop. Billy speeds to third and slides in! Beach Boy music for a few seconds.

Third base Coach Soto is grinning.

Coach Soto: "Attaboy, Billy! Remember the surfboard drill after you cross home plate."

Billy: "Yes, coach!"

The pitcher is replaced with a hard-throwing lefty closer who is a lean 6'1" and after a few warm up pitches, strikes out. The next batter, two outs. Billy is still on third.

Coach Soto: "Stay alert, Billy. Their catcher has a history of not handling fast balls out of strike zone."

Billy: "Got ya, coach."

Sure enough, after getting ahead second strikes and one ball. The pitcher threw a fast ball out of strike zone and the catcher only got a piece of the ball and the ball rolled to the backstop!

Bill took off and easily crosses home!

Beach Boy music plays again.

Billy's teammates surround him, laughing and clapping him on the back.

Coach Soto nods to Billy and looks at his surfboard, once again nodding.

Billy remembers the drill trots toward the dugout, tips his cap, bows to the crowd, and picks up his surfboard and kisses it! The crowd cheers again!

Beach Boy music briefly, the crowd once again sings along to 'Surfin Safari'!

Billy tips his hat once more and gives the crowd another bow, then enters the dugout.

The left-handed pitcher glares for a few seconds and thinks, "It's all so funny". He laughs, smiles, then settles down and gets the next two Havana players out!

Inning over! But what an inning!

Fourth inning, Havana leads three to one. La Bamba is at bat this time, their opponent decides to pitch to him! Richie Valen's 'La Bamba' plays for a few seconds – big cheers, La Bamba!

Big mistake, La Bamba hits a long double driving in a runner. The score is now four to one!

Fifth inning, Chapo comes out. Havana's relief pitcher gives up four runs. The home team is now behind five to four.

Bottom of the ninth, one out. La Bamba is walked – goes to first!

Change of pitcher! He warms up.

Coach Rios gets Billy's attention.

Coach Rios: "This Luis Sanchez throws a bunch of junk! Nothing fast, so don't get too hyped up for fast ball! Don't swing too early! Wait!"

First pitch, a wicked sinker drops into a corner of the strike zone! Strike one!

Billy is impressed. "Wow, nice pitch!"

Billy is at the plate.

Second pitch very low, Billy doesn't swing. Ball one!

Another slow pitch just out of strike zone, ball two!

Billy steps out of the batter's box thinking, "he's going inside next pitch to see if I will bite!"

Next pitch inside – Billy let's it go, ball three!

Billy is ahead in the count three balls and one strike. He knows the pitcher will most likely throw strikes. Now what pitch? Billy thinks he's going to throw another inside sinker like the first strike! Yep! Billy steps out of the box and when he goes back in to the box and digs in, Billy is five inches further away from the plate. He hopes the pitcher doesn't notice.

Wind up, throw, inside.

Pow, Billy smacks a towering home run!

Billy Lopes around the bases. 'Surfin Safari' comes on again! The crowd is singing along.

La Bamba hugs Billy as he steps on home plate.

Chapo has a big smile on his face and hugs Billy. All the teammates high-five Billy. Rios smiles and nods at Billy, then nods toward the surfboard.

Billy: "Oh yeah!"

He tips his cap, picks up his surfboard, and raises the board over his head. Music still blares another Beach Boy tune. Putting the board back, Billy pats his good luck board, tips his cap, bows and goes into the dugout! Lots of photos are taken.

The game ends six to five, the Havana stars win!!

The players stay for a half hour signing autographs and posing for pictures. A popular poster is Billy smiling in uniform, holding his surfboard. A perfect picture!

Coach Rios: "Hey Billy, La Bamba, Chapo, near first base we're having a media question and answer."

12 reporters, some with their own cameras and some with the cameramen.

Press conference:

A question from U.S.A. Today Sports to Billy:

U.S.A. Today: "Billy, have you signed up with Havana? And for how long? Can you tell us for how much?"

Billy: "Yes, I've signed with Havana for one year and I can't disclose how much money I'll be making!"

Another reporter: "Can't disclose the big bucks, eh Billy?"

Lots of laughter follows.

Reporter: "Billy, is it true you're living with Chapo?"

Chapo: "Yes, Billy and his father are living with me."

Reporter: "Are the three of you friends?"

La Bamba: "Yes, we are very close amigos!"

Reporter: "Do the three of you work on ball fields for kids?"

Chapo: "Yes, we help Mr. Wayne, Billy's dad on his new ball fields for Los Ninos."

Reporter: "Billy, have you surfed yet in Cuba and did you bring that gorgeous surfboard with you from Colorado?"

Billy: "The board was a gift from Diego, a local artist who also designed my poster!"

Reporter: "And your baseball cards?"

The reporter holds up one.

Billy laughs.

Billy: "I didn't know I had cards, please pass me one!"

The reporter walks up and hands Billy a beautiful six-color card with Billy's picture, holding his board and a baseball bat.

Billy smiles.

Billy: "Cool, I like it!"

Reporter: "Chapo, La Bamba, is it true the Yankees and Brooklyn are giving you guys offers? Do you guys have a U.S. agent?"

Chapo: "I'll let La Bamba speak for himself, but I've had no offers and have no agents!"

La Bamba: "There are rumors but no, I've never had any offers and don't have a U.S. agent either."

Coach Rios ends the press conference.

Coach Rios: "OK gentlemen, that's it! No more questions!"

Billy, his dad, Chapo, and La Bamba go out for a celebration meal, drinks and music!

Chapo: "Billy, my amigo, you were a big hit today, my big friend! I have an idea tomorrow, you have your first salsa lessons! See that young lady in the yellow on the dance floor? She gives lessons! Her name is Anita."

Billy eyes the most exotic woman he has ever seen and quickly agrees.

Anita is waved over to the table and introduced to Billy and Wayne.

Time is set for two hour lesson in the morning.

Anita: "How about you, Mr. Wayne? You will impress your wife if you can salsa!"

Wayne: "I'll take a rain check, Anita. Tomorrow I'm working on building a ball field with Chapo and La Bamba."

Anita: "See you tomorrow, Billy!"

Anita walks away, all the men enjoy the view.

Restaurant in the hills with an ocean view:

The sun is starting to set.

Chapo: "Mr. Wayne, La Bamba and I want to talk a serious talk with you!"

Wayne: "Sure you guys, what's up?"

Chapo: "Mr. Wayne, you heard the reporter asking us about offers from the Yankees and Brooklyn!"

Wayne: "Yes Chapo, I heard!"

Chapo: "Well, we lied! And we didn't lie about having a U.S. agent, we don't have one!"

Wayne looks puzzled.

Wayne: "OK."

Chapo: "We have been contacted by both teams, and also, the Mets and LA Dodgers!"

La Bamba: "Chapo and I have talked it over and we have agreed to ask you."

Wayne: "What, guys?"

Chapo: "We want you to become our agent!"

La Bamba: "Senor Wayne we trust you – you know baseball, care about kids and are a great father, or you wouldn't have a son like Billy. We love your sweet wife, Sarah Look forward to meeting your son, Chad."

Chapo: "You are the man we have been looking for as our agent!"

Wayne: "Guys, I'm a wanted man in the U.S."

La Bamba: "You are a wanted man here in Havana! Wanted by Chapo and myself."

Both La Bamba and Chapo laugh.

Wayne gets the pun.

Wayne: "Let's say I agree and guys, I'm flattered! I couldn't travel out of Cuba to make a deal for you guys."

Chapo: "So? Make them come here if they're interested!"

La Bamba: "Mr. Wayne, we can't travel but we still got some what you say nibbles – little bites from those teams. They asked who our agent was!"

The deal:

Chapo: "La Bamba and I want you as our agent with a signed agreement that will give you the power to make a deal!"

La Bamba: "We understand most agents get 20% of the deal and we both want to add some sugar to make it sweeter! We want you to have 30%. You need a bit more for money and Miss. Sarah, your sons, and all the good work you do with kids!"

Wayne: "Wow guys, this is so unexpected! You both are so very ready for the majors in the states! Aren't you both happy here in Havana?"

Chapo: "Yes we are, and we love all of our friends and relatives, but.. but with a large contract, we could help everyone here!"

La Bamba: "Maybe Mr. Wayne give you money for more ball fields for the kids!"

Chapo: "Mr. Wayne, if you make this deal, you makes us so very happy. We trust you."

La Bamba: "Also, Chapo will give you his house when we are gone.

Wayne: "Say I make a deal – how are you two going to get out of this island?"

Chapo: "We know the guys who got the Yankees new Cuban

pitcher out two years ago. 68 million contract, 12 million up front! Plenty of money for a fast boat, $400,000 for a two and a half hour trip to Miami!"

Wayne: "How's Raul Castro going to react when he learns his two biggest stars have fled. He will be so pissed he could send me back to the U.S. and I'll never see freedom again!"

La Bamba: "Well he will have one new star Billy, and your oldest Chad throws 89 – 94 is a lefty maybe that will calm him down!"

Wayne: "Chad's dream was always to play in the majors before large crowds! And make the big bucks!"

Chapo: "Havana has 22 – 28,000 people per game and as far as you say big bucks – you will have your millions to share with Chad."

Wayne: "You guys don't have to pay me any 30%. I'll do it for nothing! You guys have been so special helping me, giving me and Billy a place to live."

Chapo: "No Mr. Wayne, La Bamba and I have decided you get 30% and *that's* firm, that's it! Do we have an agent or not?"

Chapo and La Bamba stick out their hands.

Wayne shakes each man's hand and then hugs them both! Chapo and La Bamba walk onto the patio deck to smoke a stogie and celebrate the deal!

Billy: "Wow dad, what just happened?"

Wayne: "Son, your old man is now the agent for two of the hottest prospects in Major League Baseball!"

FBI Rented House:

Ramos: "Robinson, how goes the snatch and run plan?"

Robinson: "It's all set with the contractors with the fast boat.

They are good to go whenever they received the package. They will want the $400,000 up front on the night of the snatch!

Oh Ramos, here's the latest Havana Star."

He hands Ramos a copy and keeps one for himself.

Ramos: "God damn it, Robinson. You give me good news and then ruin my day with another Billy surfer dude story and pictures."

Robinson grins.

Robinson: "Well boss, might as well show you these also – similar stories, Miami papers, New York Times, U.S.A. Today!"

Ramos: "I've got a' headache, Jesus! And there's more pictures of our escaped felon with little kids and the commie, Raul Castro!"

Robinson: "I've got a feeling we are *all* going to have our nuts in a vice when we snatch Thomas!"

Ramos: "I'll take the heat – set the snatch up!"

President Raul Castro's Palace:

Raul Castro is with a Cuban security officer.

Raul Castro: "Did you hear bout the reporters at the ball field press conference?

Agent: "Si, and also the stories written after we're there! Have a coffee, let me read a few of these papers and then we'll talk."

20 minutes later, Raul Castro waves his agent to come on the balcony hands the agent a cigar – both men light up.

Castro: "I feel our two biggest star Havana baseball players will make a deal, sign a contract with the Yankees, the Mets, Brooklyn or the LA Dodgers. How can we keep them here in Havana?"

Agent: "Last time we had a star player flee two years ago. The player had super agent Lou D'Antoni make the deal. Yankees paid millions up front then agent D'Antoni had the cash to pay for a fast boat to Miami."

Castro: "Yes, and the last time Mr. Lou D'Antoni came sneaking back into Cuba, we had him arrested, spent five weeks in our worst prison and sent him back to Miami warning him if he ever came back he would do 10 years! Scared the hell out of him! What's the latest on Mr. Lou?"

Agent: "Our Miami agents say he's retired, enjoying his millions on Sanibel Island on the Florida West Coast."

Castro: "Do a check on Mr. Lou, see if he's attending any winter ball games in Fort Myers, Florida."

Agent: "Anywhere else?"

Castro: "Get a picture of any known major league agent and put their picture up at the airports and docks. Keep them out, give them at least five days in our worst jails, then send them back!

Also, see who owns a fast boat and sells fast boats in Miami. Meantime, I'll stay close to our two players who are involved in the youth baseball fields.

Do this fast, please! Let's not lose two more stars."

Agent: "Si, Presidente. Pronto."

At the Havana Airport:

Arriving alone on a flight from the Bahamas. Chad arrives and is greeted by his dad and brother! The sky is clear and sunny with a light breeze. The father and sons hug and go out into a gorgeous day.

Mike waiting with the '56 Chrysler Imperial.

Mike: "Hey Billy, Hey Wayne, this must be Chad."

The men shake hands.

Mike: "Wow, he's tall!

Chad, your dad says you play some ball and that you're a pitcher. Lefty, yes?"

Chad: "Yeah Mike, I'm a lefty!"

Mike: "How much heat do you bring?"

Chad: "89 – 94 MPH, trying to get it a little higher."

Mike: "Got some junk to go with the fastball?"

Chad: "Yeah."

Chad chuckles.

"I've got a wicked change up drop down to 68 MPH. The hitters are swinging way too early. Set em up with two straight fastballs, then drop in a slow sinker into an inside corner for a strike if he hasn't already swung either way, he's in trouble!"

Mike: "Do you have any baseball CDs of yourself?"

Chad: "Yes, I brought a few copies with me!"

Mike: "I have a special lunch planned two hours from now. If you guys are a bit hungry, we can stop and get a small taco each.

We will be dining with my boss, Senor Soto of Primo Cigar, Tony Scalia, general manager of our local Havana Baseball team. And also we will be joined at lunch by El Presidente Raul Castro who has hinted he would help your dad with some money and equipment for the kids' ballpark and playground program."

They all agree they will wait to eat later.

Chad rolls down his window and enjoys the smells and sounds of Havana. This is going to be a fine day! And wow, meeting Raul Castro! And Mr. Scalia of the Havana Baseball team!

Music coming from cafes and bars. Lots of visitors from Europe and Canada strolling, taking pictures. Vendors with their wares of souvenirs and food vendors grilling fresh vegetables and meat. The aroma of BBQ cooking made Chad hungry. He looked forward to lunch!

Lunch with Castro:

Fourth floor, dining veranda, and a large hotel view over rooftops to the ocean. Open air dining, but with shade from the sun.

Mike knows the way! He parks the car. Wayne, Chad, Billy and Mike take the elevator to the fourth floor and exit. They enter the large restaurant and are greeted by Materde, who leads the men to their table.

The table, with white linen table cloth, fresh fruit bowls, fresh flower center piece with orchids.

Materde: "Please, sit."

Waiters appear.

Waiter: "Coffee, tea, drinks?"

All in perfect English! My name is Carlos, I'll be one of your servers. Juan-"

The waiter points to another waiter.

"-will take your drink orders. There will be other servers who will wait on the rest of your party, who will arrive soon!"

Wayne: "Carlos, you have perfect English. Where did you learn it?"

Carlos: "My mom is Cuban, and I grew up in Windsor, Canada. I came here four years ago during a cold ass Canadian winter. Loved it, love the people, got this job, get to go to the beach one to two hours a day and meet nice people from all over the world!"

Chad: "Carlos, how many languages do you speak?"

Carlos: "English, of course, French, pretty well. My stepdad was French-Canadian. I needed some Rosetta Stone Spanish tapes when I first came, but now everything is good! We get a lot of French visitors and I get to wait on them a lot."

Carlos recognizes Billy.

Carlos: "Senor Billy? Could your father or Juan take our picture?"

He produces his camera phone.

Mike: "Here, I'll take everyone's picture."

Mike instructs the men to go to the balcony veranda where the ocean and palm trees will be behind the shot.

Just as Wayne, Chad, and Billy are getting set-

Castro: "Hello Mike, can Senor Soto, Senor Scalia and I get in the picture?"

Mike smiles.

Mike: "Of course, Presidente. Please, gentlemen!"

Mike: "Big guys in the back, please!"

Billy, Chad and Wayne stand behind Soto, Scalia, and Castro.

"OK, back row put your hands on the shoulders of front row. Everyone smile!"

Mike allows his boss, Senor Soto to introduce Castro and general manager Scaliato Wayne, Billy, and Chad.

Mike introduces Chad to everyone. They all shake hands.

La Bamba and Chapo arrive – more introductions and pictures with Castro follow.

Castro: "Welcome to Havana, Chad. Hope you will stay and help your wonderful father with the ball fields for Los Ninos and perhaps-"

Castro pauses.

"-play for our Havana team?"

Castro looks at La Bamba and Chapo.

"Who knows, we might have some positions open!"

Chapo whispers to La Bamba.

Chapo: "Don't panic, be cool."

La Bamba whispers back.

La Bamba: "He knows, he knows!"

Senor Soto: "Welcome to Havana, Chad. My company, El Primo Cigar is proudly the sponsor of your visit today, and later the exhibition ballgame and dinner. Your brother, Billy 'surfer dude' is hitting the ball muy bueno and is a big hit with our fans. I understand you are lefty?"

Chad: "Yes, I pitch left but bat right!"

Chapo: "Chad will be with us during warm ups before the game."

Scalia: "Chad, I understand you're a lefty pitcher. Mike told me! I'd like to see you pitch a little when we get back to the stadium and have you meet the coaches and players.

Today is just a non-league exhibition game – but we enjoy every game!"

Chad: "Sure Mr. Scalia, that will be fun!"

At the stadium:

Coach Rios: "Come over here, Chad! Meet all the players!"

Chad is introduced to all of Billy's teammates and other coaches, as well as the publicity department people who call over the team photographer.

Coach Rios: "Hey Chad, let's do a little drill, OK?"

Chad: "Sure coach, what's first?"

Coach Rios: "Chad, I know you're a pitcher, but here in Cuba it's important that pitchers can hit also! So first, you go into the batting cage and then at the batter's box, where we will do three exercise innings, OK?"

Chad has a good, solid swing much like brother and hits the ball well in the batting cage.

Chad then moves to the batter's box and hits a few balls. Coach Rios is impressed.

Coach Rios: "OK Chad, I can tell you have a good feel as a hitter! What was your average back in the States?"

Chad: "They wouldn't let us hit and used a designated hitter to bat for us. But I batted 290 in my senior year at Golden High."

Coach Rios: "Good enough, Chad. Ready to mow down some of our batters?"

Chad: "Sure, coach! Bring 'em on!"

Coach Rios: "Calling in all the players into their positions on the field!"

Chad warms up and Coach Rios and the drill begins. Chad decides to mix up his pitches fast, slow, curve sinkers and after striking out five batters, only one walk.

Coach Rios: "Chad, let's play three innings for practice!"

FBI rented condo, fourteenth floor with ocean view:

Ramos: "They raise the price on us, change the deal and are worried we won't have their money when the package arrives."

Robinson: "Yeah, that's the deal boss! Only special delivery service we could find in Cuba. These guys delivered the Yankees

68 million dollar pitcher and the Dodger's new slugger – same deal but a little less money!"

Ramos: "Sure, make the deal!"

Robinson: "Done!"

Ramos: "Another item! Lets finish up with our Miss Mole and her deal with us!"

Robinson:' Ya I brought her file with me."

Ramos: "How much money did we give our little mole?"

Robinson:*$ 56,864 in total*

A busy week on the newest ballpark for the kids. A new volunteer named Juan, who had worked with Wayne for two days approached Wayne when Wayne was alone. Juan revealed he was an independent baseball scout who worked the Islands including Cuba.

Five minutes of answering questions, Wayne was convinced the man was who he said he was! A real scout!

The two took a break and went to a tiny private restaurant and sat at a tiny, two-person table. Making sure no one was in hearing distance, Juan explained he had spoken to Chapo and La Bamba and understood Wayne was now their agent. Juan explained The Yankees wanted Chapo and the Dodgers wanted La Bamba! Both teams would pay top dollar for five year contracts. There would be guaranteed up front money for both! And because the scout understands both players are friends, he has made both deals exactly the same!

Wayne: "So Juan, what's your very best offer?"

Juan: "Both will get a five year contract, 36 million with nine million each up front deposited in a Bahama bank. Both contracts would have 18 million guaranteed. Shake my hand and with one phone call, I have authorization to put 18 million into the bank today."

Wayne smiles and thinks, "this is unreal!"

He sticks out his hand and laughs.

Wayne: "We'll need to hire a fast boat how soon?"

Juan: "This week or eight days or less. News like this seems to leak out! The Castros are going to shit a brick!"

Wayne: "Yeah, a big one!"

Juan gets on his cell phone and two minutes later, he slaps it shut!

Juan: "Within an hour, the 18 million will be in the bank via wire transfer. I understand you can't leave Cuba and neither can the two players, so I set it up with the bank for either your wife or son can withdraw funds. Once either goes to the bank, funds can be transferred more easily."

Wayne looks around the half finished ball field. Eight workers were laying irrigation pipes and building more seating. The whole contract and details with Juan had taken less than a half hour! Incredible!

Wayne: "I guess I had better inform the guys!"

Juan: "Lets set up the fast boat today! Better yet, leave that up to me! Then swear those two not tell their families, or we'll all end up in Castro's prison! After they're in Miami, they can write."

FBI rented house in Denver:

Ramos: "Where do we stand on the snatch of 'Mr. Make The Kids Some Ballparks', Mr. Wayne?"

Robinson: "Contract has been made with the fast boat and the snatch of Wayne will happen in two to three weeks! Or sooner!"

Ramos: "Sooner the better! How will the snatch go down?"

Robinson: "Mr. Wayne's car is at the new ball field and his car will be made to not be able to start! Then one of our agent's offers to give Wayne a ride home. Wayne in the passenger seat, another one of our agents behind Wayne injects him. The guys behind him gag him, hood him, put him the trunk and take him 45 minutes West to a small harbor where the fast boat will pick the package and head for Miami. Five hours, and the package is in Miami."

Ramos: "Let's speed it up!"

Robinson: "Sure, boss!"

The Snatch:

Wayne had worked since 10 AM on the latest ball field. The bulldozer with the laser had made a lot of progress in leveling the field.

It was now time for dinner and families began bringing food and drinks to the bleachers. The men were sharing cigars and sipping mojitos. All were pleased with the progress on the field.

Wayne: "Good work today, amigos!"

All the men smiled and thanked Wayne. Many were father fathers of kids who would be playing on the field!

Wayne gathered his rake, hoe, and shovel and put them into his trunk. He got into his car and tried to start the car, but nothing! Click! Click!

At Wayne's open window is one of the new workers.

Worker: "Hey Wayne, is there a problem?"

Wayne: "Car won't start!"

Worker: "Don't worry, I'll drive you home and in the morning we'll get your car fixed! OK?"

Wayne: "OK, sure let me lock it up, and thanks for the lift!"

Wayne sits up front with the new worker. Another new worker gets in the back behind Wayne.

The second man has worked nearly all day and was a good worker!

Wayne leans over the seat and introduces himself. He sticks his hand out.

The worker grabs his hand firmly and then plunges a syringe into his bicep!

What the hell is happening? Wayne feels dizzy and quickly falls asleep.

The agent drives another mile and pulls over. Wayne is bound up with duct tape. A sock was put into his mouth, made sure Wayne could breath alright and then a hood slipped over his head. The trunk opened and Wayne was placed carefully into the trunk!

Worker: "How's the gas?"

2nd Worker: "Full tank, lets' go! And I'll phone and let the boat guys know we have the package and that we'll be in their boat within an hour!"

Worker: "Half way there let's do a quick check, make sure he's OK!"

2nd Worker: "Yep."

He holds up the phone.

"Got a text! Our boat boys will meet us at about the same time as we arrive! We will text them when we are 10 minutes from arrival."

Worker: "Great, as soon as the package is in the boat and on the way, we are to text Miami the status!"

50 minutes from the time Wayne was injected, he was delivered to the tiny fishing harbor wrapped in a blanket. The exchange from car to boat took less than two minutes, with no one watching or paying attention! And no Cuban Navy!

The fast boat had two men who had raced in international fast boat races! This paid better. The men had gotten $200,000 cash the night before and had flown to the Bahamas and put all but $30,000 into the offshore bank!

Captain: "OK, let's let her rip. Not top speed, but a little under and let's look out for the Cuban Navy and later U.S. Coast Guard!"

Mate: "Yep."

He points to the binoculars hanging from his neck.

"I'll do a sweep every five minutes!"

Captain: "Make it every three minutes, let's not take any chances! We can out run everyone if we can see them ahead of time!"

Mate: "What are we going to do when we get to Miami? Deliver the package, stay a few days, enjoy some hot women and stay in some fancy rooms?"

Captain: "No my friend, we are taking the cash and heading back to our bank! I don't trust those slimy FBI guys! It pissed them off paying us! They acted like we had ripped them off."

Mate: "Hey cap, our package is waking up!"

Captain: "Stop the boat! Let's see how he's doing!"

The mate stops the boat.

The two men drag Wayne out of the cabin, take off his hood and gag.

Mate: "How are you doing? Need any water?"

Wayne: "Wayne is blinking and is thirsty. He nods yes.

The captain gives Wayne several deep drinks from a small bottle of water. Wayne is beginning to wake up!

Wayne: "Hey, I really need to pee!"

Captain: "Sure. Hey give me a hand mate, let's have him piss over the side!"

Mate: "I don't want to handle his dick!"

Captain: "Oh come on! Get a spoon out of the cabin! Ha!"

The mate goes into the cabin and comes back with a spoon. He grins.

Captain: "OK, let's get him over to the side."

The two men muscle Wayne to the side. His pants are unzipped and the spoon is used. Wayne lets loose a long, strong stream.

He finishes and looks around, his head is clearing up.

Wayne: "Hey guys, what are those tall buildings off in the distance?"

Captain: "That my friend, is Miami Beach."

"Oh no", thinks Wayne. "My life will be over once these hired guns deliver me to the FBI waiting for the escaped, convicted fugitive!"

Wayne's mind is racing, "What to do?! What to say? What to say?!"

Wayne: "Hey guys aren't you guys scheduled to bring two Cuban baseball players to Miami or Key West next week?"

Both men look at each other. How did he know about that?

Captain: "Where did you hear about something like that?"

Wayne: "Because I'm the agent for those two players and the scout for the teams in the U.S. and I made a deal for a fast boat as part of the deal. I figure you are probably the guys the scout had hired to bring those two guys next week, am I right?"

Neither man answer. They look at each other a bit stunned!

Wayne: "Look, I live with one of the players and both have helped me with building ballparks for kids and we became close friends and then they asked me to be their agent, which I agreed to! Then I met with a scout! Made a nice deal with good money for each! I agreed to pay the $500,000 for the delivery of the two players!"

Captain: "My little nephew plays in one of those parks. Are you Mr. Wayne, the North Americano?"

Wayne: "Yes, it's me. I'm Wayne and I've probably met your nephew. Do you have his picture?"

The Captain reaches in his wallet and pulls a picture of grand opening of the park with little kids, Cuban ballplayers, Raul Castro, the Captain's nephew, and there is Wayne who has his hand on the nephew's shoulder. Wow! Wayne looks at the picture.

Wayne: "Yep, that's me!"

Wayne notices the hesitation on the Captain's face and now it comes down to money!

Wayne: "Look guys, I know you have a sum of money coming if you drop me off in Miami. I'll tell you what! Take me back and I'll double what the FBI is paying and I'll add another $300,000 to next week's delivery!"

Captain: "How do we know you have the money?"

Wayne: "Keep me with you and my son will bring the cash!"

Captain: "Hey mate, let's turn this boat around!"

The Captain uses a box knife to cut all the duct tape around Wayne's body and legs.

Captain: "Wayne, we are not going to hold you for ransom. I believe you are a man of your word!"

Mate: "Is anyone hungry? We can be back in time for breakfast!"

Suddenly, Wayne was really hungry!

FBI HQ in Miami, 14ᵗʰ floor:

In a high rise room on the 14ᵗʰ floor, Senor Lead Agent Ramos and Agent Robinson waited with binoculars!

Ramos: "He should have been here by now!"

Robinson: "Depends if they were running at full throttle!"

Ramos: "Why not run at full speed?"

Robinson: "Saves fuel and easier on the engine!"

Ramos: "Huh, OK. Then at a slower speed, ETA?"

Robinson: "Some time in the next two to three hours."

Four hours later:

Ramos: "Any answer to our calls?"

Robinson: "No, and it looks like they have removed the phone's chip and we can no longer ping them!"

Ramos: "Where was the location of the boat on the last ping?"

Robinson: "Eight miles straight out from-

Robinson points.

"-here! Three hours ago!"

Ramos: "What about Google Earth?"

Robinson: "Clouds now but ETA they're heading back to Cuba, should be arriving in about an hour!"

Ramos: "Have our guys in Havana found out why the turn around? Might have been for more money. See if his rich doctor brother has pulled any large cash amounts out in the last 60 days!"

Robinson: "Sure Chief, will do!"

Ramos: "Have our guys in Havana find those swift boat turn coats and make them return our cash and explain why the turn around! God damn! Baseball dad gets away again!"

Robinson: "Well Chief, the good news is that the Cuban kids will get another ball field next week and Raul Castro will be there for opening day!"

Ramos: "Not funny, asshole! I hate Mr. Kiddie baseball felon! And I hate that damn commie even more!

The three men on the fast boat arrive in the small harbor.

The Captain addresses his mate.

Captain: "Gas her up, we will meet you at-"

He points off into the distance.

"-that little restaurant up there! What do you want us to order for you?"

Mate: "Huevos machaka and a big orange juice and a pot of coffee!"

Captain: "See you in a few! We will keep your food warm!"

Wayne and the Captain ordered their food and sipped mojitos as they waited for the mate.

Captain: "Mr. Wayne-"

He is grinning and pulls out a picture of Wayne, the kids, and Castro and hands it to Wayne.

"-I think this picture will mean a lot to you especially after today! Thank you Mr. Wayne, for building those ball fields for the ninos."

Wayne kisses the photo.

Wayne: "Thanks, Cap. I'll always keep this photo with me! It was such a special day, and your little nephew was so excited and wanted to stand in front of me for the picture."

Captain: "His father has an 8" x 10" picture of that day!"

FBI HQ 14th Floor, Miami Beach:

Ramos: "Any word from our agents about the fast boat?"

Agent: "The boat was fueled up at 7:00 AM and the boat is now in the Bahamas. The Captain and mate were seen a couple of times in Havana, then disappeared. Looks like they had a plan to escape knowing we could Google Earth satellite track them."

Ramos: "What are our chances of getting our money back?"

Agent: "Those two like to gamble and do it in Aruba at the casino there. We'll have two agents hanging out looking for those guys picking them up and jamming them before they lose our money! We have an agent watching the boat!"

Back at Chapo's:

Wayne takes a swim. The cook asks and gets a breakfast ready for Wayne.

He is on the new burner phone to the swift boat Captain.

Wayne: "Hey Cap, here's the deal! Number one, return the FBI's money right away! No delay! OK? We need the FBI to go away! Because we'll need you real soon."

Captain: "OK, will do it today! Don't know what I'll tell them about the non-delivery?"

Wayne: "Don't tell those assholes a thing! Just give them the money and when they demand an answer, just smile and walk away!"

Miami FBI HQ:

Ramos sees an agent smiling across the room!

Ramos: "Agent, what's up?"

Agent: "Just got a call from our agent in Cuba! We will have our money back today in full! The swift boat guys called and offered to return the money today!"

Ramos: "First get the money and count it, *then* ask what the hell happened!"

Agent: "Will do, Chief. I'll call you as soon as the money is secure!"

Three and a half hours later, the money is returned by the mate to an FBI agent in the Bahamas.

The agent calls Ramos.

Agent: "Hey Chief, got our cash back, all dollars are here!"

Ramos: "What did he say when you asked, why they didn't deliver our package?"

Agent: "Chief, he didn't answer, just smiled, shrugged and walked away!"

Ramos: "Damn! We'll never use those guys again!"

The Captain informs Wayne.

Captain: "The money has been returned!"

Wayne: "Are you ready to deliver two packages?"

Captain: "Yep, let's rock n' roll!"

Wayne: "Any worries?"

Captain: "Naw, once we get three to four miles out, nothing can catch us!"

Wayne knows the team has four days off and decides it would be a good time!

He takes Chapo's extra car to the stadium and walks over to Chapo and La Bamba.

Wayne: "Hi guys, let's have a serious dinner at La Bamba's tonight. Do not, *do not* speak of this to families, girlfriends, to *anyone*, OK?"

The two men agree.

Wayne: "I'm not kidding, we can all end up in Raul's prison! End of your Cuba baseball career! So keep quiet, we'll let your families know! And first thing, get a couple of burner phones for each of you!"

Wayne is still worried one of the players would call a girlfriend.

Wayne: "Tell you what guys, give me the names and phone numbers of who you want to talk to and I'll get each a burner phone and you can talk to them in two to three weeks, then we will get them new phones and will do this over and over! OK?"

The men both nod yes!

Wayne's new burner phone buzzes.

Wayne: "Hello?"

Caller: "Hello, can you have two packages delivered, same place at 8:00 PM?"

Wayne: "I most certainly can! Guys, we are on for tonight!"

Chapo: "I need to hug my amigo good bye."

Wayne: "Sorry Chapo, no can do. Too dangerous! Guys, let's get out of here right now!"

La Bamba: "Not even to change clothes?"

Wayne: "Nope, just do it at your house and no talk in front of the cook and server! Let's enjoy the meal, swim, and head out to make the 8:00 PM meet!"

The men were very careful, but excited. This would mean leaving family, friends, fellow players, and their amigos!

And perhaps even the women they had fallen in love with.

Both were young. La Bamba, 25 and Chapo, 26. Both while in the pool talked quietly about things they would like to do in the U.S.

Chapo: "I want to see Papa Hemingway's house in Key West and Jimmy Buffet's bar!"

La Bamba: "I want to spend a week in Disneyland and see Hollywood and Malibu."

Chapo: "Me too! Let's see a few places together before we split up and go to our teams, OK?"

La Bamba: "Sure, let's ask Mr. Wayne to set this up! And let's try to see the Statue of Liberty and New York City!"

Chapo: "Let's enjoy Miami Beach! Dance with some beautiful girls! Mr. Wayne said we could have four to five days in Florida and I have two cousins working at the Sugar Reef Grill in Hollywood, Florida! I'd like to see them and have a meal with them! It's been four years since they got out! Here's a picture of my cousins with the whole staff at Sugar Reef Grill."

La Bamba pulls out a picture from his wallet.

La Bamba: "I don't know if we are going to be taken to Key

West or Miami, but either way let's agree to have one long meal with your cousins at the Sugar Reef Grill."

Chapo: "Yes, my amigo!"

Two days later, the two men were left at 4:00 AM in Key West and were met by two of Wayne's friends from Denver, who had flown into Key West two days prior.

The four men had a huge breakfast, drank mojitos and went to a smoke shop to burn some good Cuban cigars.

The four shared a large Magnom of Dom champagne in celebration!

One of the Denver men handed the two ballplayers their new phones and each got a small leather pouch with $10,000 for spending money!

Denver Friend: "Let's call Wayne, hey guys?"

Chapo & La Bamba: "Yeah, let's call Mr. Wayne!"

Chapo dialed Wayne's number and put the phone on speaker.

Wayne: "Hello guys, hope you are enjoying yourselves. What are your plans for tonight?"

Chapo: "La Bamba and the whole group are going to Jimmy Buffet's for a big meal and music! Tomorrow morning we go to Papa Hemingway's museum!"

Key West had made Hemingway's home in to a tourist attraction and three tours a day went through the famous man's home!

La Bamba: "Does Cuba know that we're in the U.S. yet?

Wayne: "Not that I know of, but I'll get a copy of the Miami Herald in the morning!"

La Bamba: "El Presidente, will how you say, shit a brick!!"

Wayne: "Yeah guys, I'm thinking towards a meeting right away – with Senor Raul!"

Chapo: "Good luck with that! I hope you don't end up in prison!"

Wayne: "I think I'll be OK for a while."

Wayne thinks this because of Raul's support for the kids' new ball parks and playgrounds, and the recent photo ops with Wayne!

Wayne calls the Presidente:

Wayne: "Hello, Mr. Presidente!"

Raul Castro: "What's new, my friend?"

Wayne thinks, "If only you knew!"

Wayne: "Are you available for photos at the newest ball park tomorrow?"

Raul Castro: "What time?"

Wayne: "How is 9:00 AM?"

Raul Castro: "Can we make it 8:00 AM?"

Wayne: "Sure, I'll set it up! Will you need anything to eat?"

Raul Castro: "No, I've got an engagement at 10:00 AM with a breakfast and brunch."

Wayne: "Also OK if I bring both of my sons for the photos?

Raul Castro: "Si, it's OK and make sure Chapo and La Bamba are there!"

Wayne tries to keep his voice calm.

Wayne: "Si, Presidente!"

Wayne knows time is short before the stuff hits the fan!

The next day at 7:45 AM at the newest ball field, Wayne, Chad, and Billy along with some of the local volunteers and 15 neighborhood kids are there when Raul Castro and Mr. Soto arrive! The local paper and the Miami Herald reporter and TV crew were also there!

Wayne shakes hands with all including Raul Castro.

Raul Castro: "I've heard Senor Wayne that your oldest son will soon start for the Havana Stars?"

Wayne: "Yes, Chad will pitch for three innings this Thursday!"

Raul Castro: "Where are the ball players today?"

Wayne: "Sorry, I didn't invite them."

Raul Castro: "Well Chad and Billy and the head groundskeeper are here!"

Miami Reporter: "Billy, do you have a your surfboard with you?"

Raul Castro: "Billy, please get your surfboard for the nice reporters!"

Billy: "Sure, it's back at the house. Be back in 15 minutes!"

Billy trots off.

Castro smiles.

Raul Castro: "Well, two Americans on my favorite team."

He chuckles.

"Fidel family is amazed and follows Billy's news everyday, and now Chad! We will all be at Thursday's game!"

Wayne thinks, "Oh brother.. cat will be out of the bag very soon!"

Photos are taken. Everyone is very happy except for Wayne, who's stomach is in knots.

Billy and Raul Castro pose together with a bat and the surfboard. He pops a bicep and Castro is photoed feeling Billy's muscle.

Raul Castro looks Wayne in the eye.

Raul Castro: "Looks like we need some new muscle on the Havana Stars!"

Wayne thinks, "Does he know?"

Wayne: "Cuba is now my home!"

Raul Castro: "Be loyal my friend, to your new home!"

Wayne thinks, "I hope my new home won't be a Cuban prison. Does he know yet? Why the loyalty remark?"

Castro had imprisoned thousands in his many years in power!

Would Wayne's work on the kids' ball fields be enough protection to save him from Raul's anger over losing two more stars?

Raul Castro: "It would be good if your oldest does well in his pitching! Fidel's family is following your son's playing very closely!"

Wayne suspects Raul knows his two stars have fled!

Raul Castro: "Fidel's family and I will be at this Thursday's game! Will Chad be pitching?"

Wayne: "I believe he's pitching three to four innings and Billy is playing the whole game!"

Raul Castro: "We will see you Thursday. Why don't you sit with us and Mr. Soto?"

Wayne: "Yes, I'll join you Thursday!"

The next day, Wayne, Billy and Chad got to the stadium. Something was wrong! The players were looking at a newspaper.

Wayne thinks, "Oh no, cat's out of the bag!"

Coach: "Hey you three, come over here! Have you guys seen the front page of the Miami Harold?"

Wayne, Billy, and Chad take a look.

There on the front page was Chapo and La Bamba drinking champagne at Jimmy Buffet's in Key West. Long story about the guys big contacts with the Yankees and the Dodger's.

Both men looked so happy! The coach smiled and looked at Wayne and his two sons. All three shared a large group hug. Their two friends were safe!

Havana Dreams

Printed in the United States
By Bookmasters